RUGBY RIVALS

RUGBY RIVALS

Mike Levitt

James Lorimer & Company Ltd., Publishers
Toronto

James Lorimer & Company Ltd., Publishers acknowledges funding support from the Ontario Arts Council (OAC), an agency of the Government of Ontario. We acknowledge the support of the Canada Council for the Arts, which last year invested $153 million to bring the arts to Canadians throughout the country. This project has been made possible in part by the Government of Canada and with the support of Ontario Creates.

Cover design: Gwen North
Cover image: Shutterstock

9781459414945
eBook also available 9781459414938

Cataloguing data available from Library and Archives Canada.

Published by:
James Lorimer &
Company Ltd., Publishers
117 Peter Street, Suite 304
Toronto, ON, Canada
M5V 0M3
www.lorimer.ca

Distributed in the US by:
Lerner Publisher Services
1251 Washington Ave. N.
Minneapolis, MN, USA
55401
www.lernerbooks.com

Printed and bound in Canada.
Manufactured by Friesens in Altona, MB in September 2020.
Job #269557

For Loll

Contents

1 Tight GAME

Today is a perfect day for rugby. A drizzle of rain has turned into a steady downpour and the grass is torn up into a field of mud. This is a game we have to win. It's halftime and we're down 10–8. The pressure is on and I can't wait to get my hands back on the ball.

The ref blasts his whistle to start the second half. We're playing against the Fairview Falcons, and their white jerseys are covered in muck. They kick us a deep one. Our fullback stumbles in the mud. He makes a fingertip catch and boots it out at our forty. At the line-out I take my spot at the very back. I'm praying our hooker will throw the ball in straight.

"Right down the middle," the ref warns him.

Coach Kanavula wants me to get out quickly and help take down their powerhouse inside centre. The guy's nickname is Muscle because Fairview recruited him out of the weight room. When he's running right at you, it's like trying to tackle a truck.

Our whole team knows Fairview's plan. Get the

ball out to Muscle. In the first half he scored all their points. I need to sprint from the back of the line-out and try to get a piece of him. The only way to stop this guy is a shoestring tackle. I have to hit him low and wrap up his ankles.

Fairview wins the line-out. Sure enough, the ball goes to Muscle. He runs straight at our inside centre, Travis Peters. Travis has been getting run over all day. He stands his ground, even though he's already got a black eye and a fat lip.

Muscle drops his shoulder and thunders forward. Travis dives for Muscle's knees. He can't hang on, but it's enough to make Muscle stagger a step. I launch myself shoulder first and clamp both arms around Muscle's shins. He crashes face first into a puddle of sludge and the ball squirts loose.

For the next twenty minutes they keep us pinned in our own half. They either feed Muscle or kick the ball deep. With only minutes left, there's a scrum on their forty, our put-in. My team looks over at our captain, Logan Reed. Logan looks more like a volleyball guy than a rugby player. But he's a smart fly-half and a good captain.

We need to score. There's only minutes left. And this is the very last game any of us will play for the North Shore Spartans.

"What's the play?" I ask Logan.

He holds up two fingers like a peace sign and

everyone knows what's on.

Fairview has a hard-nosed scrum and we've had to grind it out every single set. We know this one is going to be just as tough.

"Crouch," calls the referee.

The props and hooker are already bound. That leaves our locks, who drop onto their knees. I nudge up right next to them and drop both my knees and a fist to the soggy turf.

"Bind," says the ref.

I reach across the back of our nearest lock and grip a handful of his mud-slick jersey.

"Set!"

I jam my right shoulder up under the cheek of our loose-head's butt. It's a solid fit.

Our scrum-half, Liam Grant, flips the ball into the tunnel and we heave forward. My back is ramrod straight. My legs flex like steel springs. All eight of us scrummers surge as one. It's a twelve-hundred-pound shove, and we barely move forward. But it is just enough for our hooker to get his foot on the ball and win the strike.

Liam takes a quick look down at the ball. Our number eight is doing a good job of controlling the ball at the back of the scrum. Liam plucks the ball from the number eight's feet and puts up a monster box kick. It's super high and more than thirty-metres deep. We race forward in a wave, hoping to get our hands on the ball. But the kick is just a bit too long. Fairview's winger makes a good catch and punts it out of bounds.

"One minute," says the ref.

"Red thirty-five!" Coach Kanavula bellows from the sideline. It's our line-out twenty-five metres from the goal line. All of us know the next play.

I hope it works. It's up to me.

This time I set up at the front of the line-out. The plan is a simple back wind. The throw goes long to Reese Rankin. He's called the Giraffe, because he's the tallest guy on the field, all arms and legs.

I take off racing for the back of the line-out. Reese catches the throw-in and drops me a perfect pass. I charge into open field. I sidestep their fly-half and jink inside a flanker, so there's only the fullback left to beat. I sprint to get past him, but he launches a tackle and gets both arms around my waist. I pump my legs with the ball clamped safe to my chest.

Their flanker catches up and hammers me hard. He wraps me up, ball and all.

As I'm going down, I pray for support. Coach Kanavula says I've got a great offload. Sometimes when there are two or even three tacklers on me, I find a way to squeeze out a pass.

Logan is right there. He stretches out a long volleyball arm and snatches up my little pop pass. He powers two long strides and dives over the goal line.

"Try scored!" The ref blasts his whistle.

We're ahead 13–10!

"What a beauty!" I throw myself at Logan and nearly knock him over with a bear hug. A bunch of the guys leap on top of us. We all crash to the ground and there's a dog pile right there in the mud. That's the thing I love about rugby. We might not all be best buddies. But sometimes, like right now, it's the best. Like we're all brothers.

It's like we've won the World Cup. The win makes us second-last in the Okanagan North League. *Not* last.

2 On EDGE

In the change room after the game, we've got a surprise for Coach Kanavula. Coach Kanavula is the biggest Fijian man you'll ever see. He's also got the biggest smile you'll ever see. And he's my favourite coach ever. He's standing at the front of the room, beaming, rubbing the stubble on his jaw. The game ball is secretly passed from hand to hand. When Coach Kanavula smiles down at his clipboard, I scrawl my message on the ball. *Thanks for a great year, Coach. Sam Brewer*

"Coach Kanavula," Logan calls out. "We've got something for you." Logan makes his way to the front and hands him the ball. Coach Kanavula shakes Logan's hand, then takes a minute to read our messages.

"I guess we're all going in different directions," Coach says. He looks up. I can see the sadness in his eyes. "I want to wish every one of you guys good luck in your new schools. I'm going to be teaching at P. T. Phelps Elementary. But that game is a great way for me to remember the North Shore Spartans."

North Shore Junior Secondary is closing at spring break. The pulp mill shut down last year and people started leaving our part of town. A few months ago, the school's shop wing burned down, and the Kamloops Board of Education said, "That's it. No rebuilding."

"You know where you're going yet?" I ask Logan.

"Rivers High," he says. "Me and the Giraffe. You?"

"Rogers, I guess." I grab the back of my collar, strip off my mud-soaked jersey and give it a toss. It lands with a splat on the floor. Like everyone else, I waited for a letter from the school board. They're splitting us all up based on our addresses. You get assigned to a school. No one gets a choice.

"What if one of us has to go to the Heights?" jokes little Manny Baines. He's our manager.

"Are you kidding?" Liam holds two fingers to his temple and pretends to shoot himself.

"I wouldn't go if it was the last school on the planet," says Logan.

Everyone hates Rosedale Heights Secondary because it's up on Snob Hill. Last time we played there, someone wrote *GHETTO* on the side of our bus. Sure, we're from the North Shore, but it was still a lousy thing to do.

"Anyone who goes to the Heights is a total jerk!" Logan spits in the garbage.

In the shower I let the hot water numb my aching shoulders. The mud on my knees and elbows slips off in gobs. I watch a little river of sludge swirl down the drain.

Out in the parking lot, my mom and Pop give me a wave. Pop is my grandfather. Mom says he's got something called dementia. It makes him forget the easiest things, and sometimes he gets really confused. Most of the time he's okay. Sometimes he's totally embarrassing.

"Great game, Sam!" Pop sticks out his big square hand. He's a big-boned guy with a buzz cut. I shake his hand and he pulls me in for a hug. My cheek scrubs on his whiskers and he gives me a couple of massive thumps on the back. "You threw some great hits." Rugby was always Pop's game, too.

"Good game, Sam." Mom pecks a kiss on my cheek. People say I look like Mom. We're both tall and freckled. But in my first rugby game I broke my nose, so now it's bent to one side. Like Pop's, not Mom's.

"Your mom busted me out," smiles Pop. He likes to joke about his retirement home, Pringle Ridge. Pop calls it *Wrinkle* Ridge.

Last year Pop was starting to forget stuff. Mom found a carton of milk in his cupboard. He let the bathtub overflow. Then his place nearly burned down when the bacon caught fire. So Mom moved him into the retirement home. I think it's expensive. Mom's got a little cleaning business, but I think Pringle Ridge sucks up a lot of her money.

"Let's get some lunch," Pop says. "My treat."

My heart sinks. I love the old guy, but the dementia thing puts me on edge.

We get to Subway just in time. A team of ten-year-old soccer girls comes in right behind us. Pop is at the front of the line. I'm next, then Mom.

A kid with braces and *SKIP* on his name tag asks Pop, "What will you have, sir?"

I count fifteen people waiting in line behind us.

"Meatball, please." Pop smiles.

"Whole wheat, honey oat, Italian, nine grain or parmesan?"

"Hmmm." Pop rubs a palm over his bristled head.

"How about nine grain?" Mom speaks up over the noise of the soccer kids. "You like that."

"Sure." Pop nods.

"Six or twelve?" Skip asks.

Pop looks confused. "Just one," he says.

"Six-inch!" Mom is nearly shouting to beat the racket.

"White or cheddar?" Skip asks.

Pop cups a hand behind his ear so he can hear. "Sorry?"

"Cheese?" says Skip.

"Yes, please," Pop nods.

"White?"

Pop looks at me for the answer. His hand is rubbing his head at full speed.

"That's fine," I say. I can see Pop is right on the edge.

"Toasted?" Skip asks.

The soccer team celebration is bouncing off the walls.

"Toasted?"

Pop's face is red. "I don't want toast." He clamps his hand to the top of his head. "I want a meatball sandwich!"

This is not good.

"Veggies?"

The soccer kids start a drum roll, slapping their thighs and drumming the tables. One of them comes out of the bathroom with her face painted green. It must be some kind of silly initiation. They all laugh. Someone whistles and the shriek ricochets off the walls.

"Veggies?" Skip yells at Pop.

Pop is wide-eyed. "Those." He stabs a finger at the glass cover.

Skip puts spinach on top of the meatballs. I hold up a hand but it's too late. Pop hates spinach.

"Not that!" Pop yells. He turns and barges through the lineup. And right out the door.

3 The First CUP

By the time Mom and I catch up, Pop is in the middle of the street. He's got one hand up like a traffic cop. He's holding up a half-dozen cars. Someone blasts a horn. A guy in a dump truck hangs out of his window and yells, "What, are you crazy?"

I'm red-faced, totally embarrassed and praying no one I know is watching. Mom shoots out onto the street and takes Pop by the elbow. She hustles him back onto the sidewalk.

Pop is furious. "Cucumber!" He stomps his foot on the ground. "That's all I wanted."

"It's okay, Pop." Mom pats him on the shoulder and leads him to our van. "Jeez," she says, "you should get a job directing traffic." Mom is like that. So calm under pressure that she can crack a joke. She opens the passenger door for Pop.

Our van is puke yellow and rusted out. It's Mom's work van for her cleaning business. It's the ugliest vehicle in the entire world.

"We'll get some lunch at home," Mom says.

Pop slouches into the passenger seat and folds his arms tight across his chest. It's hard seeing my Pop losing it. He used to be kind of cool. Smart and funny.

Soon, Mom pulls the van up to our place. There's a 1998 Ford Ranger pickup in our driveway with weeds growing up around the tires. Pop and I love working on it. When I'm sixteen, I'm going to drive it.

Mom and I live in a tiny one-bedroom basement suite, but we're hoping to get something bigger. Mom sleeps on a pullout couch in the living room. Every morning we stash her blankets and pretend it's a living room again. It's a secret. I pray no one ever sees Mom's bed in there. What would they say? *Sam's family is so hard up they sleep on the couch.*

Mom fries up Pop's favourite grilled cheese. As soon as I smell margarine hissing in the pan, my stomach growls. I slice pickles and see that Mom has made the sandwiches thick with cheddar cheese. I guess she wants to make it extra special.

Pop wolfs his first bite and says, "Really good." He points across the table. "Can you please pass the ketchup, Dave?"

Pop calls me Dave sometimes. That was his brother's name.

Pop taught me how to kick a ball and ride a bike. He showed me how to cast a fishing line and how to bait a hook. We caught about a million trout at a place on the Thompson River called the Sunday Hole. So it bugs me when he calls me Dave.

Mom says I just need to remind him.

"I'm Sam," I say. "Your grandson. Remember?"

Pop raps his forehead with his knuckles. "Yeah," he says. "Sam."

We have maple walnut ice cream for dessert. Pop's other favourite. Then Mom says it's time to take Pop home, as she wipes a bit of ice cream off his chin.

"Back to Wrinkle Ridge, home of the rich and famous," he jokes. "There's daytime TV, the Go Bus and Saturday night bingo."

"Hang on a sec." I disappear into my room and grab our big canvas laundry bag. Mom works long hours, so I try to do my part. That means doing the laundry.

As soon as we step into the lobby at Pringle Ridge, I can smell the place. There's a whiff of cleaning products but there's something else. It's like a big pot of soup on the boil. No matter what time of day it is, it always smells like old people's onion soup.

We take the elevator to Pop's little room on the second floor. Mom helps him get his coat off. Then she gives him the pill he always takes.

"That was one heck of a game," Pop says. He shuffles over to the bookshelf and picks up a framed photo. "Nothing quite like rugby." Pop looks at the photo. It's a black-and-white of him standing between two other guys. They all wear muddy jerseys and have their arms locked around each other. Pop has his head wrapped in a bloody bandage, and one of the guys has cotton jammed up his nose. The third guy has a trickle of blood down his chin.

Pop taps a finger on the little gold plate at the bottom of the photo. "Know what it says right here?"

"I know exactly what it says," I say. "*He who sheds his blood with me today shall be my brother. The Brotherhood.*"

"And isn't it true . . ." Pop gazes at the picture dreamily. "That's Willy O'Brian from Ireland and Tomasi Vulla from Tonga."

I've heard their names a million times. In the old days Pop travelled the world and made tons of friends playing rugby.

"Any town, any rugby club in the whole world," Pop says, tapping a finger on the photo. "Just knock on the door and you've got a whole new batch of buddies." Pop stares off in the distance for a moment, like he's remembering.

"Rugby is like that," he says. "It's a brotherhood. No game like it."

I've heard Pop say these very same words since I was a toddler.

"And that was a great game today." He picks up another photo. "Now this was a grand old team."

I've seen this picture a million times, too. And I've heard the story a trillion times.

"The Quinton Cup." Pop runs a finger over the photo. "That's us back in '72, first year of the Cup. We were the champs. Best day ever."

I know the story word for word, but I don't mind hearing it again. Pop gets a real twinkle in his eye when he talks about the Cup.

"That '72 team, we had ranchers' kids and bronc busters. A pair of brothers from the boxing club. Half a dozen hard-nosed hockey guys — and a little Shuswap kid played on the wing. That kid could outrun a rabbit."

In the picture, Pop is sitting in the middle of the team with the Cup on his knees. He's the coach. All the guys are wearing old-school cotton uniforms with the collars popped up. When I was little, I used to dream that I was in the picture. Pop was always so proud of it.

A few years ago, Mom filled me in on the full story. Turns out that Pop was the first coach to organize a North versus South Okanagan Junior Championship. He bought the Cup himself and named it the Quinton Cup.

Mom told me that Quinton was the kid who could outrun a rabbit. He was killed in a car crash a month before the championship game.

"You guys got a shot at the Cup this year?" Pop rubs a hand over his head like he's polishing it.

I'd love to tell him we do. But I can't lie to Pop.

"North Shore Junior is closing. I'll end up going to Rogers," I say. "Not much chance of winning the Cup over there."

"Oh, yeah," Pop says. "So who's going to win?"

"Rosedale Heights is my guess," I say. "The Heights has already got first place in the Okanagan North."

"They play the winner of the South." Pop shuffles over to his big reclining chair. "Is the Heights still a senior school? Eight to twelve?"

"Yup," I say, "and nearly two thousand kids."

Pop eases into his chair and holds his old team picture right in front of his nose. "Game day." His voice isn't much more than a whisper. "The day an ordinary guy can make history."

I've heard Pop say that before, too.

"But wouldn't it be something . . ." There's a far-off look in his eye.

"What?" I've got a pretty good idea of what he's going to say next.

"To win the Cup." Pop has melted into his chair. "The Quinton Cup, one more time."

I wish I could do it. I wish I could somehow get the Cup back in Pop's hands.

4 Crosstown RIVALS

On the way home, back on the North Shore, Mom pulls the van up to Pinky's Laundromat. Pinky's is in a rundown area called the Corridor. There are a lot of people in the Corridor that Mom calls down-and-outers. I keep my distance, and normally people go about their business. The Corridor isn't as bad as they say. It's just a lot of poor people.

"Thanks, Sam." Mom loves it when I do the laundry. She ruffles my hair as I step out of the van. "See you at home."

I use the big canvas bag to shove the laundromat door open. There are bright lights inside, and the linoleum is mostly worn through. It always smells like wet socks.

At the back of the place is a skinny guy in a long grubby coat. He's bent over one of the machines, wiggling a coat hanger in the coin slot trying to get at the loonies. The only other person there is a preppy little guy about my age wearing a Billabong hoodie.

"You can't do that, man," the little guy is saying to the coat-hanger guy. "I just put my money in there."

The coat-hanger guy stands up. "You need to shut up." He points the chunk of wire at Preppy.

It's been a few years, but I recognize the coat-hanger guy. "Hey, Trevor," I call. I walk right up with the giant bag still hoisted on my shoulder. He looks up and searches my face, trying to remember me.

"The YMCA," I say. "You were my swim coach."

He looks down at the coat hanger and stuffs it under his coat. "You got an extra buck?"

"I'll give you a buck if you stop trying to wreck the place," I say.

Trevor holds out a grimy hand. "Deal." He takes the dollar, sneers at Preppy and hustles out the door.

"That was your swim coach?" Preppy asks.

"One of them." I smirk. "The other one was a Hell's Angel."

"Yeah, right." He combs his fingers up through his hair. He has perfectly spiked bangs. They stand straight up.

I heave the bag onto the counter and ask, "You new around here?"

"Just doing the wash." His eyes dart back and forth. He reminds me of a nervous bird. "I'm Sparrow," he says.

Sparrow, I think. *It suits him perfectly!*

"My real name is Dave Wong," he explains. "But everyone calls me Sparrow."

"Sam," I say. "What are you doing on the Flats?"

"They're doing big-time renos at my school. Water's off. And no chance my mom wants thirty muddy rugby jerseys at our house. North Shore is the only place in town that still has a laundromat."

All three of his dryers are tossing blue and white jerseys. I recognize them. "Are those Rosedale Heights colours?"

"You got it." Sparrow salutes me like an army guy. "Rosedale Rebels rugby manager at your service."

"No kidding," I say. Sparrow seems like an okay guy. But I remember *GHETTO* on the side of our bus.

"Pretty nice up there?" I clink a few loonies in a machine.

"Pretty *nice*?" Sparrow combs three fingers up through his perfect spikes. "It's the snottiest place ever. Kids with BMWs, million-dollar houses and everyone bragging about spring break in Jamaica."

"So why be the manager?"

"Everyone has to play a sport at the Heights. My only way out is to be team manager." He stabs his fingers into his spikes again. "Do you think I like taking stupid rugby stats in the rain? Not a chance." His eyes flit around the room again. "Know what?"

"What?"

"I just try to survive. Place is full of jerks, so I'm a bit of a loner. The Heights isn't an easy place to make friends."

He starts pulling jerseys out of a dryer, folding and stuffing them into a Rosedale duffle bag. His eyes flit back and forth. It seems like he's never still.

"Hey, Sam," he says as he slips the bag off the counter. "That coat-hanger guy —"

"Yeah?"

He wraps both arms around the bag and lugs it off the counter. "I owe you one."

5 Special REQUEST

Somewhere in my messy locker there's a math textbook. Somewhere under the rugby ball, cleats, scrum cap and towels. I dig through notebooks and binders crammed one on top of the other. The morning announcements come on. Now I'm *officially* late.

"If you are still unsure of your transfer school, the lists are posted at the office." The secretary's voice crackles through the overhead speaker. "Anyone with library fines please see Ms. Davie. And could Sam Brewer please go to Coach Kanavula's office as soon as possible."

What's this about? I wonder.

When I get to Coach's office, I see the door is open a crack.

"Sam," he says, "come on in." He rubs a hand over his big square jaw. He always looks like he could use a shave. "Have a seat."

His office is more of a mess than my locker. Stacks of files spill across his desk. The shelves are jammed with books and binders. I sit in an old-school straight-back wooden chair. It has a jacket and towel hanging off the back.

"I'll get right to it, Sam." His voice is deep and smooth. "Rogers is not the best school for a guy like you."

"How come?" I ask.

"You're a grade nine kid with a ton of potential. With your instinct at the breakdown. Plus, you're really developing a great offload. You need top-notch coaching to reach your next level."

"Okay . . ." I say it like a question.

"You're the real deal," says Coach Kanavula. "Your attitude and your sportsmanship. You're always the first guy to help somebody up off the deck, no matter which team he's on. And you play the game with a smile on your face!" He slaps the top of his desk. "No one says *spirit of the game* like Sam Brewer."

"Thanks, Coach." I say. I never know what to say when someone is gushing compliments.

"You need to be in the best program we can get you in." Coach Kanavula's deep voice is serious, like he's trying to drill in his point.

"Like where?" I think I know the answer.

"I could write a recommendation letter for you."

"Aren't there rules about which school you have to go to?"

"Special request," he says. He places his massive hands palms down on the desk. "I've already made a call."

"Which school?"

He's leaning back, trying to be relaxed about it. I'm perched right on the edge of my chair.

"Rosedale Heights," he says.

★ ★ ★

By suppertime I've thought about it from a dozen different angles. I've decided. I can't go to the Heights. I'd hate it. It would never work.

I'm standing at the stove stirring a big pot of macaroni. It's steaming up the kitchen window. There are sausages in our big frying pan, spattering hot grease all over the stove.

Mom comes in from outside. "Smells good," she says. She's wearing makeup and her best shoes.

"Special occasion?" I ask. "You're all dressed up."

"I just had an interview," she explains. "Tallman and Schuster in the big law office building. They need a cleaning service. Could be a really big contract."

"Then it has to be gourmet Kraft Dinner." I hold up the ketchup bottle. We sit at the table and I tell her the news. "Coach Kanavula called me into his office, said I'm the real deal and he thinks I should go to —"

"He sent me an email," Mom cuts me off. "Tells me Rosedale Heights has a great program." Sounds like she got the same talk I did. I'm sure Mom knows the place is full of rich kids, but she doesn't say anything about that part of it.

"I can't go there." I drop a heavy glob of KD on my plate. "It's all rich kids."

Mom shrugs. "Kids are just kids, though. Right?"

"You don't get it." I drag a chunk of sausage through the ketchup.

"But your coach said the place has connections. You want to move up. More Heights players get recognized than —"

"I know," I cut her off. "But we don't have the money."

"Money for what?

"Stuff."

"Like what?" She takes off her jacket and hangs it on the back of her chair.

"Like clothes and stuff. And how do I get six miles across town every day?"

"We can get you a student bus pass. And something new at the mall." She smiles. "Maybe new jeans."

She doesn't get it.

6 Done DEAL

After we've done the dishes, I'm sitting on my bed and my phone pings. It's a text from Logan:

just want to say we had a good run

I text back.

It was fun all right — good luck at rivers

We played a whole season together. Now it seems like it's all over in one text. But I remember what Logan said about the Heights. Anyone who goes there is a jerk. Maybe the word is out. Maybe he knows about my talk with Coach Kanavula.

He sends one more text:

maybe see you on the field one day

I'm staring down at my phone wondering what I should text back. It rings. It's not a number I recognize.

"Hi, Sam. Coach Roberts here," says a nasal voice. "Rosedale Heights."

"Hi." I sit straight up on the edge of my bed.

"I heard you're interested in coming up to the Heights," he says.

He has caught me totally off guard. What do I say? "Thinking about it," I say. It comes out in my super-high nervous voice.

"We run a great program up here. And I guess Coach K told you we could sure use a guy with your skill set and your offload. And I heard you're still a grade nine. You'd be a solid fit on our Junior Team."

I don't feel solid. I feel queasy. My heart is hammering and I'm starting to sweat. There's a pause and it seems like it's my turn to say something. "What's your schedule like?" I stammer.

"Well, we've made it through. Won the North Okanagan. Probably going to be playing Western Park in the final. And at the end of the season we've got a match with Bedford School from England." He pauses and lets that last part sink in.

I'd *love* to play against a team from England. Win or lose, it would be the best! Not many guys get a shot at an international. Pop would be all over it. "Oh, wow," is all I manage to say.

"There's an intersquad game over spring break," he says. "Want to play?"

"Sure." I don't even think. I just say it.

"Glad you're on board!" He sounds totally stoked. "There's a bit of paperwork," he adds. "No big deal."

There's another pause. I should say something but I'm not fast enough.

"We need to do an official transfer," he tells me.

"Okay." What was I *supposed* to say?

"Done deal!" he says, "Call me anytime. Congratulations! See you on the pitch, Saturday noon."

Holy crap! is all I can think.

★ ★ ★

For the next couple of days, I'm so freaked out I can hardly eat. *I'm going to play in an intersquad at the Heights!* I keep thinking. How did I get myself into this? Each time I picture stepping into the Heights change room, I feel like I might barf. I can't go there wearing my ratty gear. And I'm sure as heck not wearing my North Shore Spartans jersey.

It's all a mistake.

After a while I work it out. I figure out a plan.

I sit on the edge of my bed and stare at Coach Roberts's number. All I have to do is tell him I'm not going to Rosedale Heights. I've told Mom how sketched out I am. She says it's still my choice.

I'll tell Coach Roberts that I've decided to stick with Rogers. "Sorry about the mix-up," I'll say. It's simple. Just a three-minute call and I'll have it over with.

I hold the phone and stare at it. My palms are clammy. My thoughts are racing. I need to call before I chicken out. I stand up and punch the numbers.

It rings twice before he answers. "Roberts here."

"Hi, Coach Roberts," I say. "This is Sam Brewer."

"Good news at this end, Sam," he says before I can say anything else. "Your transfer is moving smooth as silk."

"That's the thing." There's a second or two of silence. "I'm not so sure."

"I know how you feel." His nasal voice is totally calm. "It's okay to be nervous. But you're a perfect fit. No worries."

"What I'm thinking, though . . ."

"One thing we need, Sam," he jumps in, "is your size. For jersey and shorts."

"Probably a medium," I say. "Maybe a large jersey."

"Excellent," he says. "I'm glad you called. It's perfectly normal to be a bit anxious at this stage in the game. It's a new team, all new guys. But tell you what — play in the intersquad on Saturday. Then decide."

7 Enemy TERRITORY

By Saturday I'm so tense that brushing my teeth makes me gag. My stomach rolls over every time I think about stepping into the Rosedale change room. I'm a mess.

I get off the bus a couple of blocks from Rosedale Heights. I take a deep breath and start walking. When I look up at the school, my legs turn to rubber. The main building is three storeys high. It's made of solid stone, and there are vines growing up all over it like something out of *Harry Potter*. The clock tower stares down at me. Tall trees and clean-cut shrubs stand guard. There are even rows of flowers. The only flowers we had at North Shore Junior were dandelions.

I walk up the sidewalk and around the side of the school to the fields. There's a clean, fresh-cut-grass smell in the air. The field is perfectly lined and the corner flags all stand at attention. The change-room door is closed when I step up to it. I can hear the rumble of voices inside. I stand face to face with the Heights crest on the door. In big block letters it says *REBELS ONLY*.

I ease the door open and step inside. Half the guys stop talking. They're already in full uniform. I must be late. No one says a word to me, or even nods. They just look at me. I wonder if I should walk back out.

I have entered a long room with lockers and benches on either side. The players are crowded shoulder to shoulder, and there's no place for me to change. With every step I take deeper into the room, more heads turn. The place goes quiet. It's like I'm on stage.

This is a huge mistake, I think.

"Here." Someone throws me a blue jersey and a pair of socks. It's Sparrow, the guy from the laundromat. He points to the very back of the room where there's a bit of space to change, then walks away.

When we get out on the field, a team of three coaches with matching Rosedale Rebels golf shirts are waiting. The one who introduces himself as Coach Roberts doesn't really look like a rugby guy. He's got a slicked-down, stringy comb-over and a beach-ball belly bulging under his shirt.

"Good morning, men," says Coach Roberts. "It's a great day for a game of rugby." He reads the names for three teams: A, B and C. I'm the last name read out, as open-side flanker on the C Team.

I can tell from looking around that the C Team is the underdog. It's junior rugby, but half of our backs are still in grade eight. A few of the forwards are tall and flagpole skinny.

"We're going to play a round robin," says Coach Roberts. "Each team gets two short games."

For game one, the C Team, my team, plays the A Team. We line up against them, ready to play. The A Team is all tall, athletic guys wearing the sharpest blue jerseys and crisp white shorts. They're the pride of the Rebels.

The whistle blasts to start the game. Our fly-half puts up a perfect kick. The ball floats high and I sprint downfield after it.

One of their guys calls, "My ball!"

I know if I time it just right, I might get under it. At the last second, I leap high into the air. I snatch the ball with both hands and hit the ground running. Their fullback gets his arms wrapped around my waist, but I keep pumping my legs forward. I'm dragging the guy like he's an anchor.

Then someone hits me hard around the thighs. Another player's shoulder cracks the side of my head.

The ref chirps his whistle. "High tackle!"

I clamber to my feet. For a second I see spots. I can feel a trickle of blood on my ear, but I don't touch it. Best to act like it's no big deal.

"A bit of blood there," the ref points to my ear. "Can we get it cleaned up?" He calls for the trainer and there's a pause in the action.

The guy who hit me with the high tackle is a prop. He's a South Asian guy and one of the biggest scrummers on their team. He says something to a guy with an arm sling who's standing on the sideline.

"Welcome to the Heights," says arm-sling guy. The two of them whisper to each other, then burst out laughing.

Screw you! I'm thinking. That was just a little knock. Just enough to get me fired up.

Arm-sling guy makes a big show of pretending to sniff the air. "I smell ghetto." He smirks and points a finger at his sling. "This comes off in two days, Brewer."

"Keep your head up," says the South Asian guy.

Part of me wants to ask, "What's with you guys?" But I ignore their threats and jog towards the play. I've got two new enemies. But I'm not sure why.

Our fly-half surprises me again. He's a short, round little dude, but he nails a champion kick to the corner and out of bounds. That makes it our line-out ten metres from their goal line. Our throw-in is crappy. One of their super-tall locks tips it to their side. But no one grabs it!

I bust through the line. The ball takes a wonky bounce and I snatch it one-handed. The goal line is only steps away. I charge forward. Three metres out, I dive, stretching forward with both arms extended. Their hooker hammers me in mid-air and we crash to the ground.

"Tweeeet!" sounds the whistle. "That's a try!"

Five minutes into the game and I've done it! The kid from the wrong side of town scores on the mighty Rebels!

"Nice hustle," Sparrow says from the sideline. Then he quickly looks away. The round little fly-half gives me a thumbs-up, but no one else says a word. My teammates turn and jog to centre. I look at Coach Roberts. He's writing on his clipboard.

That's it? I wonder.

The rest of the game is one-way traffic. By halftime it's 24–5 for the A Team. All I've been able to do is make solid tackles and try to get my hands on the ball. In the last minute of the game, the A Team's beefy number eight picks up a ball from the back of a set scrum. He's a monster running right at me. I dive low and make an ankle tackle. He thumps to the ground.

I'm totally spent, gasping big breaths on all fours, when the whistle tweets to end the game. Finally. I've made a million tackles, but no one says a thing. It's like I'm the invisible man.

In our next game, the C Team gets thumped by the B's, 15–0. At the end of the practice Coach Roberts smacks his clipboard on his thigh. "You guys played some great rugby today," he says. "And there was some outstanding teamwork."

I feel like I played some great rugby, sure. But *teamwork*? I was alone out there, just trying to prove myself.

Rugby Rivals

I skip the shower and head for the bus. Walking past the school, I look at the size of the building and wonder about next week. My first day of classes. The empty windows glare down at me.

8 Rosedale SUCKS

The next day, Pop is over for Sunday dinner. The spicy smell of Mom's spaghetti and meatballs fills the room. The three of us sit jammed at the tiny kitchen table.

"So what's the plan?" Pop slices a meatball in two.

"The plan?" I pause with a dangle of noodles on my fork.

"Tomorrow, isn't it? First day at the Heights?" he says. "You need a plan."

"Just be myself," I say.

"Good idea," says Mom. "You'll make friends in no time."

"Fly under the radar," Pop says. "You want to blend in."

"Exactly," I nod. But I'm not even sure what to wear. And it isn't like I have a lot of choices. At the North Shore it was just jeans and a T-shirt. But Mom sent me to the mall yesterday with enough to buy a Billabong hoodie. That's what Sparrow was wearing. Hopefully it will help me blend in.

"I've worked a whole lot of different jobs," Pop says. "Oil rigs. Logging camps." Pop points his fork at me. "To get on with a new crew, I've got two rules. Shut up and work hard."

I just nod. It sounds like a pretty good idea. Pop might not be with it all the time, but he still has good advice.

Pop points across the table. "Pass the . . . uh . . ." He's forgotten the name of something.

"The pepper," Mom says as she hands him the salt and pepper.

"Well, there you go." Pop bumps the heel of his hand on his forehead. "Taking advice from an old fart who can't remember the salt and pepper."

After supper Mom brews a batch of coffee in a saucepan. Our drip coffee maker broke down. Mom was going to buy a new one until I splurged on the Billabong hoodie.

★ ★ ★

The next day I get off the bus a block from the school. My legs are like rubber, and the feeling I might barf is right there at the back of my throat. When I get close to the school, it looks even bigger than it did on Saturday. There's a mega-wide set of stairs leading to the front doors. I'm so nervous I can hardly breathe. Dozens of kids are funnelling up the stairs. I slip through the big double doors. No one seems to notice me.

Rosedale Sucks

Inside, the ceilings are high and the halls are filled with kids crowded shoulder to shoulder. I find my way to the office and get in line. There's a group of senior girls in front of me. They're chatting about spring break. They went to Mexico, Hawaii and Costa Rica. Every one of them is tanned, and they all look like they're ready for a fashion show. I've scrubbed my runners clean but I can't hide my George jeans from Walmart.

My first class is English with Mr. Morris. I step into the classroom and the teacher gives me a warm smile. "Good morning," he says. His voice is soft. He has heavy-rimmed glasses and his eyes are kind. "You must be Sam."

"Morning," I say. "Yeah."

"Welcome to English nine." He hands me a book and says, "Good timing. We're just starting a new novel. Oh, and I'm one of the counsellors. My office is at the end of the hall if you need anything."

Mr. Morris seems like a pretty nice guy.

I take a seat near the back of the room. Mr. Morris teaches some vocabulary that's in the novel. He reads the first chapter aloud and asks us to read to chapter four for homework. And that's it! My first class at Rosedale is over. No one seemed to notice that there's a new guy from across town.

My next class is Social Studies. I slip in the rear door. The teacher is organizing papers on a table at the front. She's got grey hair and glasses around her neck like someone's grandmother. There's a seating chart on the sideboard and my name is on it. I move to my seat by the windows.

A bunch of kids come through the door, talking and laughing. They glance at the seating plan and go to their desks. The guy with his arm in a sling from the intersquad comes in. He glares at me. It doesn't take a genius to figure it out. He's going to be my number-one person to avoid.

The beefy South Asian guy lumbers along behind him. He's the guy who gave me the 'welcome to Rosedale' high tackle. The two of them stand towering over the teacher and looking at the seating plan.

"Oh, come on!" Arm-sling guy picks up an erase brush. He holds it by his name on the seating plan as if he's going to erase his name.

"Hey, hey!" The teacher wags a finger but has a little smirk. "What do you think you're up to?" She puts on her glasses.

"Come on," he whines. "I hate the front." He holds the brush right over his name.

"Mr. Bittner . . ." The teacher threatens arm-sling guy with a pointed finger and looks at him over her glasses.

"What if I change it?" Bittner wipes half a letter off the end of his name.

"Bam!" She punches a fist into her opposite hand. "Straight to the office." It's all in fun. But when she points to his desk, he seems to know he's played it as far as he can.

He turns and goes to his seat. The big guy follows.

The teacher starts calling out names for attendance. My name is third on the list. "Sam Brewer?" She scans the room looking for me.

I raise my hand halfway up.

Everyone turns to look at me. I feel my ears getting hot.

She beams a big smile. "Welcome to Rosedale, Sam. I'm Miss Benz." She turns to the class and says, "Sam has transferred from the North Shore." She holds her index finger to the side of her head like she's thinking. "We're doing the chapter on map projections. Where did you leave off at NSS?"

"Climate change," I say. Everyone is still turned in my direction. "I did a PowerPoint on . . ."

Before I can finish, Bittner cuts me off. "Do you still live over there?"

I nod.

"The Corridor?" blurts beefy guy. "You live in the Corridor?"

Part of me wants to tell him that the Corridor is just one tiny part of the North Shore.

"Mr. Bittner! Mr. Dhaliwal!" Miss Benz says their names like a warning.

I'm looking down at my desk and praying she just keeps taking attendance.

"Are you in a gang?" Bittner asks.

"Okay." Miss Benz holds up both her hands for him to stop. There's no sign of her smile. "That's enough."

"I'm just asking," says Bittner.

"*We* don't know," says beefy guy. Dhaliwal.

Bittner gives me a big fake smile. Dhaliwal shrugs and tries to look like he's totally innocent.

"Open your textbooks to chapter nine," says Miss Benz.

I don't have a textbook. I'm not going to ask for one. The last thing I need is more attention.

9 Total SHAME

At lunch I find a spot in the cafeteria at the end of a long table. A group of younger guys a few chairs down ignores me. I spot Sparrow in the lineup with earbuds in. I wonder if he'll see me.

"Can I just wipe that up?" A girl with a shiny, jet-black ponytail and a blue school apron is pointing at a little puddle of juice in front of me. When she leans forward to wipe it up, her hair brushes my shoulder. I get a whiff of something nice. Shampoo, I think. It smells like apples.

"Thanks," I say.

She wipes the whole area in front of me. Her arms are a rich copper brown and they're ripped with muscle. There's a scrape halfway along one forearm.

She sees me looking at her scrape. "Mountain biking," she says. "Missed a corner."

"Must have really hurt." I'm trying my best to keep her talking.

"I did it on Saddleback." She keeps wiping. "Up a bit off the River Trail."

I think Saddleback might be on my side of town, but I don't know for sure. I'm not a mountain bike guy.

I lean back on two legs of the chair. "You ride a lot?" I'm trying to look relaxed. This girl has my heart thumping double-time.

"I do." She stops wiping. "I'm in your Socials class. There's a lot of jerks in there."

I can see she's feeling bad for me. There's sadness in the way she looks at me. She starts wiping again, moving away. She gets to the far end of the table and I feel like I'm going to lose her.

"See you in class." I hope I didn't yell. I said it pretty loud.

She stops and smiles at me with her head tilted a bit to one side. I don't know a lot about girls, but I know she's giving me a legit smile. Like maybe she actually *wants* to see me in class. She gives me a tiny wave, then turns and walks into the kitchen. For the very first time at Rosedale, I'm feeling okay. Next Socials class I'll find out her name.

I'm not really hungry. But I start eating my apple and look at my phone. I'm just trying to look like I fit in.

Then I spot Bittner, Dhaliwal and a hefty red-haired guy. They've come through the double doors into the caf. I slouch down and try to hide behind my phone. They sit across the room, but Bittner spots me. They all look over. Just as I'm about to get up to leave,

Bittner gets everyone's attention.

He stands up and calls out, "Here are your lunch-hour announcements." He starts reading from a piece of paper. "All bus students, there is a change in today's schedule."

It seems like a weird way to do announcements. But there are a lot of weird things at this school.

"The bus to Walmart will leave at three fifteen," he says. A few people giggle.

What's funny? I wonder.

"A fashion workshop will take place in room one twelve." A few more people laugh. "Anyone wearing George jeans or last season's Billabong is invited to attend."

Dhaliwal points at me and says, "And we'd like to welcome the new guy from North Shore Secondary."

Every single person in the caf turns to look at me. My face flushes.

"The next bus for the Corridor is leaving immediately," yells Bittner.

Suddenly a beefy hand closes on my shoulder. I didn't notice Dhaliwal coming up behind me. He holds me down as Bittner saunters over. "Better not miss that bus, Sam," he says.

Dhaliwal's hand tightens, squeezing until I can feel my bones scrape together.

"You don't want us to have to walk you out of here," Bittner snarls. "I might have to kick that

George-jeans-covered butt." I can see by the gleam in his eyes that he means it.

I grab my stuff and bolt outside. The whole place is laughing. I march straight towards the bus stop.

"Hey, Sam," someone calls from behind me.

If it's one of those guys still hacking on me, there's going to be a fight. I turn with my fists clenched. It's Sparrow, jogging to catch up.

"I forgot to give you this." He holds up a slip of paper.

If this is a joke, Sparrow is in for it.

"Locker assignment." He tries to hand me the paper. "Combo is on the back."

"I don't need it." I turn and keep walking.

"Every rugby guy gets a full-size gym locker."

"I'm out of here."

"Bittner's an idiot." Sparrow has to hurry to keep up. "And he's super pissed. He was starting open-side flanker until he sprained his wrist. Now you're going to take his spot."

"Whatever." I keep walking. But I want to hear what Sparrow has to say.

"It's a fight for the open-side flanker spot!"

I can tell Sparrow likes the idea. He's not a big Bittner fan.

"Seriously, man." Sparrow is hustling along right beside me.

"I'm on the C Team," I remind him.

"Not for long."

I want to know more, but I can't let Sparrow see that. I keep up the pace.

"I'm the manager, dude. I *hear* stuff," says Sparrow. "I've heard the coaches and they all agree. They say you've got killer instincts at the breakdown and you'll be moved up. You'll make it to the A Team. I know it."

I'm still going so fast that Sparrow has to jog every once in a while to keep up.

"But watch out for Bittner," Sparrow warns. "He's got a full-on mean streak."

"I'm starting to figure that out," I say.

When we get to the bus stop he says, "I've got to go back." He nods towards the school.

"The girl in the caf," I ask. "The one wiping tables. You know her?"

"Brooke Baptiste," he says before heading back to the school. "Only First Nations kid in the whole place."

"What do you know about her?"

Sparrow turns and calls over his shoulder. "I heard she's a car thief."

10 PAYBACK

I wish I'd stood up to those guys, said something back. Even if it would have meant a beating. Maybe all I need to do is face them down and it would be over. It seems dumb to give up on everything. Rugby. School. And even dumber to give up on Brooke Baptiste.

When I get to Pringle Ridge, Pop is in the dining hall. The place is nearly empty, so I'm guessing lunchtime is almost over.

"Dave," says Pop when he sees me. "You get the truck running?"

"I'm Sam," I remind him. "Your grandson."

He studies me. His spoon is frozen halfway up to his mouth.

"Sam," I tell him again. "I play flanker." Rugby sometimes brings Pop back into the real world.

He glances up at the clock. "Why the heck aren't you in school?" I think he's *back with it*, as Mom would say. Pop goes back and forth from totally out of it to with it in the blink of an eye.

"Want some?" Pop tips his bowl for me to see inside. It's fruit salad. There are bits of peach and pear, and half a pale cherry.

"Sure." I know the routine. Family can have a dessert from the side table. I get a little bowl full of fruit and one of the tiny teaspoons.

"How's the new school?" Pop asks.

"It's totally upscale," I say. "But it's not like I'm making a bunch of friends. Matter of fact, a couple of guys are hacking on me straight off."

"Sounds about right," says Pop. "Always got to test out the new man."

I'm too embarrassed to tell him the full story. "But I quit." I look into my bowl. "I'm going to Rogers."

"One bad morning," says Pop, "and that's it?"

I nod and move the chunks of fruit around with my spoon.

"Seems like this place has got the best of you," says Pop. "There are all kinds of battles in life. Some you fight and some you walk away from." He leans across the table and looks me straight in the eye. "Sounds to me like you might be walking away a bit early."

I just stare at my spoonful of fruit.

"Think about it," says Pop. "There's maybe more than one reason this is worth fighting for."

Pop is bang on. "Yeah," I agree. I haven't told him about Brooke Baptiste, but he's got me thinking. What if I go back tomorrow? What's the worst that could happen?

"When's the next rugby?" he asks.

"Practice after school."

"You should go." Pop nods. "Just get right back on your horse and ride."

★ ★ ★

Just as the three o'clock bell rings, I push open the change-room door. It's early and the room is empty. I go to the whiteboard and read the posting for today's three intersquad teams. I'm open-side flanker. This time on the B Team.

Practice starts with a stretch. The A Team captain, Will Nakamura, is the sharpest fly-half in the league. He leads the stretch for all of us. More than fifty players.

Bittner has his forearm wrapped. But he is in full practice gear, ready to play. Dhaliwal stands right next to him. They look at me, whisper and laugh. I wonder what kind of plan they've got for me. I imagine it's going to be something offside.

Coach Roberts calls us in under the posts and says, "We'll start with contact drills. Then the intersquad games will run fifteen minutes each way."

In the first drill, eight guys set up along the sideline, each with a crash pad held over a ball.

"Hit the pad low and drive the man off the ball," Coach instructs. He pats down his comb-over and slaps the clipboard on his leg. "It's a basic clear-out."

We line up to face the players holding the pads. Bittner has a pad, and I end up in his lineup. He's about my size.

When it's my turn, I rush forward and smash my shoulder into the pad at knee height. Bittner absorbs the hit and slides the pad over my back. He drops all his weight on me, pad and all, smothering my head and shoulders into the pitch.

"I want you off this team," says Bittner, low enough that no one else can hear. "And if that takes putting you in the hospital . . ."

A couple of minutes later, Coach Roberts calls, "New men on the pads!"

I grab a pad. Bittner lines up against me. He's got a snarl on his face and his fists are clenched.

He takes off at half speed. Then he drops low and explodes. He drives his shoulder into the pad and locks his hands behind my knees. I can't step back. He keeps driving until my back thumps the grass and my head hammers the turf.

"Had enough yet?" mutters Bittner as I scramble to my feet.

"Easy there, Bittner," one of the coaches calls out. "We're all on the same team here."

It sure doesn't feel like it, I think.

After the drills, we start the intersquad games. A few minutes into the A versus B game, on the B Team we're already down by a couple of tries. Bittner is on the A Team, but he and I haven't crossed paths. A minute later the A Team is attacking thirty metres out from our goal line. There are a couple of guys from each team fighting to drive over a tackled player who has released the ball on the ground. Their team is winning the ruck. The scrum-half scoops up the ball and pops it to Bittner.

Bittner charges forward and runs over one of our guys. He straight-arms another and is thundering for the goal line. I'm sprinting across field. I've got him in my sights.

Ten metres out from the line, I hammer him from the side. It's a powerhouse tackle. I've got him wrapped up, ball and all, and I'm driving him towards the sideline. As he's stumbling forward, going down, I slip a forearm on the back of his neck. As we crash over the corner flag, I ride him into the turf. Bittner slams face first into the dirt.

The ref blows the whistle. "Out of bounds! No try."

I jump up. Bittner lies there for a moment.

Then, very slowly, he clambers to all fours. His nose is bleeding. Blood drips off his chin. He touches the blood then stares at his bloody finger like he can't believe it.

11 RUMOURS

The next day I'm at my locker between classes. Part of me is proud that I got back at Bittner. But part of me is drowning in doubt. Coach Roberts never said anything, so I guess he thinks it was legit.

But I know it wasn't. Coach Kanavula said I'm Mr. Sportsmanship, the first one to help a guy up. Now I give a guy a bloody nose. I feel like I've broken an unwritten rule.

Brooke Baptiste is at her locker halfway down the hall. I know she walks this way to get to her first class — I just have to time it right. Out of the corner of my eye I see her shut her locker door and start walking my way. My heart thumps.

As she goes by, I pull my head out of my locker. "Hi," I say.

"Hi," she waves.

"Do you have that Socials outline?" I hope I don't sound too lame. "I think I lost mine."

The second bell rings. There's two minutes to get to class.

"Somewhere." She stops, but glances down the hall towards her class. "Can I get it to you later?"

"Sure," I say. "Yeah."

What am I thinking? Like she's going to hang around and be late because I ask her for some stupid outline? Dumb plan.

"I heard you tackled Bittner," she says. "Gave him a bloody nose."

I nod. I guess the word is out.

"What's a late hit?" she asks

"What? Where did you hear *that*?" My voice has jumped up an octave.

"That's what Dhaliwal said." She shrugs.

"It was a clean hit," I say. "Nothing late about it!"

"Okay." She shrugs again like she doesn't care one way or the other. Then she flashes me her smile, gives a little wave and hurries away to class.

I hope she doesn't think I'm a cheap shot.

A couple of guys I don't know are walking past. One of them gives me a thumbs-up. Does everybody know?

All day long it seems like people are giving me a second look. And most of them are smiling. I hear a couple of guys whispering in English class.

"New guy gave Bittner a bloody nose."

"Bittner probably had it coming."

When I get to my locker at three o'clock, I freeze. Someone has smeared a sandwich all over the front of my locker. Mustard and mayonnaise are caked around the lock, and a piece of loose-leaf paper is taped to the door. *WATCH YOUR BACK, CHEAP SHOT.*

★ ★ ★

The next day, as soon as I walk into Social Studies, Dhaliwal flips me the finger. There's another new seating plan. Bittner and Dhaliwal sit near the front, a few desks apart. I have a good view of them from the back. While Miss Benz is writing on the whiteboard, they're busy texting. Something makes Dhaliwal laugh and he turns to grin at me.

Brooke is a few rows over. She has her head down and is copying the notes off the whiteboard.

"Here's a list of topics for our new interview assignment." Miss Benz points to the board. "Everyone will need a partner."

Brooke turns in her seat and looks right at me. She raises her eyebrows like she's asking to be partners. I nod. She makes my heart race.

"Go find your partners." Miss Benz claps her hands like we're in grade four. "Off you go." Once everyone is moving, she has to yell over the noise. "And everyone pick your topic!"

I hurry to get across the room.

"Start planning your questions," shouts Miss Benz.

I sit in the desk right next to Brooke.

"What about number three?" Brooke points to the choices on the board. "About homeless people."

There's so much talking that I can hardly hear her. "Sure," I say.

Brooke says, "We could do it like a TV news interview."

The kids next to us are making a racket, and people are still dragging chairs around. "What?" I ask. Maybe she'll lean closer.

"Hang on a minute." Brooke goes to the front of the room and talks to Miss Benz. Then she walks back and picks up her stuff. "Come on." She starts walking towards the door. I follow.

"I told Miss Benz we'd do better out here in the hall," Brooke says. She walks around a corner and sits cross-legged on the floor.

We're in a little window alcove a few doors down from the classroom. I slide down the wall and sit cross-legged next to her. She flips back her glossy hair and I get a whiff of shampoo again. This time it smells like coconut.

"The thing about Bittner," I tell her. "It was a totally clean tackle. I might have ground his face in the dirt a little. But it wasn't a late hit."

"I believe you." She touches her hand on mine. "Rumours are crazy around here." She scoots herself around so we're face to face. "The stuff about me is nuts."

Our knees are touching. I hope she's doing it on purpose.

"I can't keep up with half the things they say about me," she says. "But I did do something really dumb. Mandy — she's my best friend back on the rez, Blue Mountain Reserve out in the Chilcotin. I lived there until I was ten. Well, Mandy and I took her stepdad's car out one night. Just for a quick rip."

Brooke is looking right into my eyes. She has long, thick lashes.

"When it was my turn to drive," she says, "I crashed into a stop sign. The stepdad charged me. Said I stole the car."

"That's harsh."

"Totally," she says. "As part of the court thing, they said I had to live with my dad. They said Mom isn't a responsible parent. And it's kind of true. Mom's a bit off the rails."

"And what's your job in the caf about?" I ask.

"I do it twice a week so I don't have to play a sport."

"What about rugby? You *must* love rugby." I wiggle my eyebrows up and down.

"Bunch of guys in the mud." She tries to frown but her eyes are smiling. There are sunlit flecks of green all around her pupils. "I mountain bike." She says it like a challenge.

I've got an old beater bike but I don't mention it.

"I ride every day." She gives my knee a playful slap. "I'd kick your butt."

"Oh, you think so?" I laugh.

"We should race," she says.

"We can race," I say, "but only if I get a big head start."

By the time the bell rings, it seems like the class has flown by. We haven't said a word about our project. But I've learned a lot about Brooke Baptiste.

12 Full OUT

The next day is the last practice before the Cup final. All fifty-one of the Rebels are sitting crammed into the change room. We're waiting to hear who will be on the A Team.

All Coach Roberts has to do is clear his throat. Everyone shuts up and looks at him. "We're still deciding on starters for the Cup final." He runs a hand across his comb-over. "There are a few positions you guys will need to fight for."

It's so quiet you can hear the hum of the heating system.

"It'll be Matt Carver or Aman Jalmar for tight head. Raj Gill or Matt Romano at fullback.

Then, open-side flanker," he says. "Shawn Bittner or Sam Brewer."

"I got it," Bittner says from the back of the room. A few guys chuckle, but it's pretty tense. Everyone in the room knows there's a battle between us.

When we finally get outside, there's a refreshing

drizzle of rain. Sparrow walks by with a bag of balls and tosses one to me. "There's going to be head-to-head sprints," he whispers. "So save some energy for the end of practice."

I give him a thumbs-up.

Coach Roberts chirps his whistle and we circle around him. "We're going to run through everything," he says. "Our defensive shapes, offensive patterns and all the set pieces."

Bittner is behind me. "Good luck, dickweed," he whispers.

He thinks he knows this stuff better than I do. Maybe he does. I've been trying to memorize it all, drawing x's and o's and going over it with Sparrow. All I can do is hope I get it right.

"We'll start with kickoffs," announces Coach Roberts. "Put them up high," he tells Will Nakamura, "and short enough so guys can get under the ball."

Will nods. He's a pinpoint kicker.

Coach gets us set up in groups of four. I'm in the first group. Will puts up a kick and I race downfield with my eye on the ball. I leap up and snatch it out of the air.

"Great take!" says Coach Roberts. "Just like that, boys."

Bittner is in the next group. He leaps and snags the ball out of the air, just like I did.

"Perfect!" says Coach Roberts.

I'm surprised how high Bittner jumps and how good his hands are.

We run through set scrums, counter attacks and our defensive patterns. Half the time Bittner is at open-side, half the time I am. Luckily, I remember everything I need to. We set up for a line-out and Coach Roberts throws in a twist. He puts me at blind-side flanker and keeps Bittner on at open-side.

First line-out, Will makes the call. "Two fifteen, blue forty-five."

The ball will be coming to me. The guy behind is supposed to boost me. It's Bittner. *He has to do his job*, I think. If he drops me or screws up it will look bad on him.

The hooker throws. As soon as I jump, I can tell it's going to be a tiny bit short. I'll need to really stretch for it. Bittner does a good job of hoisting me up. At the top of my jump, the ball is almost in my hands. Then Bittner does it. He twists me. Not enough for anyone else to notice. Just enough that I can't get both hands on the ball. I try a one-hand grab, but I can't quite control it. The ball slips off my fingers and hits the ground.

"You've got to stay square to the ball," Coach Roberts calls out from the sideline. "Keep your shoulders square, Sam."

If I complain I'll look worse than I already do. I bite my lip.

"Tough luck," says Bittner. "Maybe next one." He slaps me on the back like we're old buddies.

I feel hot blood rush into my cheeks. Both my hands clamp into fists.

The practice is coming to an end when Coach Roberts blows his whistle. "Everyone on the goal line."

This is it, I think. *Head-to-head sprints.*

Coach Roberts puts us in groups. Props will race props. Wingers against wingers. Flankers against flankers.

The butterflies are flying around in my gut as I watch the first sprints. When Bittner and I step up to run, Coach Roberts says, "You two guys are making it tough. Both great players."

I crouch, legs flexed.

Coach Roberts says, "Ready, ready, go!"

I spring off the line. Bittner is right behind me. I can feel him gaining. Then he's right next to me. We cross the line and he's just a nose behind.

"I had a terrible start, Coach," Bittner whines. "Slipped my first step."

"Let's do it again," says our coach.

I burst off the line again. This time Bittner stays right with me. At the finish he's ahead by a hair.

"Nice try," he whispers so only I can hear.

"One more for good measure," Coach Roberts says, pointing back to the starting line. A couple of guys cheer. Everyone loves a good battle.

"What?" Bittner has his hands on his knees. He's gasping. "I thought that was it."

"Endurance," says Coach Roberts. "It's all part of the game."

We crouch to start. Bittner is still sucking wind.

"Ready, ready, go!"

I blast off the line. My arms are pumping and my cleats are ripping up sod. Bittner is puffing behind me. I finish a couple of metres ahead.

Sparrow meets me at the finish line with a bit of a smirk. "You had time to stop and tie your shoe," he jokes. But doesn't look up from his clipboard.

At the end of practice, Coach Roberts calls us all in. "I'll list the starters the morning of the Cup final."

All I can do is wait.

13 Try-Saving TACKLE

The Cup final is only two days away and I'm trying to do everything right. I've been drinking lots of water, eating a bunch and trying to get plenty of sleep. The night before the game, I go to bed at nine-thirty. But I can't sleep. I've got a million thoughts racing around. I know that Western Park is a super tough team. They're undefeated in the Okanagan South. Some of their playoff scores were crazy — 20–0, 30–0. They beat A.L. Christian in the final by fourteen.

And I can't stop thinking about Brooke. Maybe I could ask her to a movie. I wonder if she notices my sad George jeans. I haven't worn the Billabong hoodie since that day in the caf.

My phone pings. It's a text from Sparrow.

You r starting

I kick off my covers. I text, *what??? How do u know I'm the manager!!!*

★★★

Try-Saving Tackle

The day of the big game, I'm so stoked that I'm out of bed by seven. By game time the grandstands are overflowing. Dozens of fans are waving blue-and-white flags.

From the change room I can hear air horns blast and the school's jazz band playing. The smell of Deep Heat and nervous sweat is thick in the room.

Coach Roberts calls us all in and says, "This is it, boys. This is our day. Two thirty-minute halves." He pauses and wipes a hand over his comb-over. It's slicked right down for the big game. "We've got one hour to make our mark in the history pages."

The field is in perfect shape. Overhead there are fat white clouds, and a little breeze is blowing. I'm totally pumped. I'm dying for the opening whistle.

The ref finally blasts his whistle to start. Western Park kicks off high and deep. Our fullback Matt Romano backpedals to get under the ball. Just as he's making the catch, he gets smacked with a thumping tackle.

Western Park rips the ball away and one of their players boots a perfect grub kick downfield. The ball takes a series of little bounces, end over end. It hops up to waist height, then plops to the grass and dribbles over our goal line. A pack of us race to get there. I'm a step behind the Western Park winger. He dives for it. I'm right on his tail, but he gets a hand on the ball.

"Try scored!"

We've been playing less than a minute and they're up by five.

A few minutes later they kick a penalty. It's a perfect kick off the tee that sails dead centre between the posts. Another three points scored, and we're down 8–0. This isn't the way I pictured it. But it's only eight points. We're pinned behind our twenty-two-metre line for most of the half. Every time we boot the ball downfield, they hit us with another counterattack. Each time I make a tackle, I pop up and fight to get my hands on the ball. But I get driven back or wrestled off it.

Two minutes before halftime. Western Park is ten metres out from our goal line. The ref calls for a Western Park scrum, their put-in. They win it with a rock-solid scrum. Their scrum-half fakes likes he's throwing a pass, a gap opens in our defence and he darts through. He spins out of a tackle and dives for the goal line. He's soaring through the air when I hit him with a flying tackle. There's only one thing I can do. It's totally legal if I try to punch the ball out of his arms.

I swing an uppercut at the ball. My fist is right on target and I hammer the nose of the ball. It pops out right in front of the scrum-half's face. He clambers for it with both hands flapping in the air. One hand looks like it might have slapped the ball to the turf. He skids to the ground with me on top of him.

Did he score?

The fans are silent.

The ref is right there.

"Knocked on," he yells. "No try!"

"Great hit, Brewer!" Coach Roberts shouts from the sidelines. He makes a circle with his thumb and forefinger. "Perfect."

Bittner is standing next to him. He's punching his fist into his palm. I'll bet he'd rather see Western Park put another try on the board than me make a try-saving tackle. Screw him!

A little way down the sideline I get a glimpse of someone waving a little blue Rebels flag. It's Brooke!

14 Try SCORED!

Halftime in the change room. I sit at the end of the bench sucking big breaths. It's 8–0. We've been playing defence the whole first half and I feel like I've been run over by a bus.

Coach Roberts says, "We've got the breeze this half, boys. I want you to kick over their defence and into the corners. And remember, boys, a kick is only as good as the chase."

Sparrow gives me a bag of ice. "Eleven," he says, tapping a pencil on his clipboard. I know what he means. I've already made eleven tackles. I put the ice bag under my jersey and rub it on my shoulder, letting the melt trickle down my back.

Coach Roberts starts reading the changes for the second half. "Gill in for Romano. Carver for Jalmar."

I'll probably be subbed out. I'm expecting it.

"No changes in the back row," Coach says.

That's me. No sub.

This is supposed to be a team game, but all I'm

thinking about is my *own* game. I wonder what Coach Kanavula would think. So much for me being the whole package.

Bittner is across the room glaring at me.

In the second half, Will Nakamura places a few deep kicks. Our defence is solid and we throw a series of tackles that knock them back. It's twenty-five minutes before we get into a good attacking position. A Western Park guy grabs me by the head and shoulders and twists me off a ruck. They get called for a neck roll. Will takes the penalty kick twenty metres out and right in front of the posts. It's just a chip shot for Will. Finally, we're on the board. Three points to their eight. But everyone knows the clock is ticking.

"How much time?" Will asks.

"Five minutes," says the ref.

With every second, I feel the game slipping away. I can see doubt in the faces around me. The Rosedale fans are hushed. There are no air horns, and the jazz band is silent.

Two minutes later there's a line-out at centre field. It's our throw-in and Coach Roberts hollers from the sideline, "Black forty-five!" He's calling for only six men in the line-out. He wants me to set up right behind our centres in the open field.

We win the line-out and the ball goes out to Will at fly-half. He fakes a reverse with the inside centre, who is cutting back towards the line-out. Then he throws a long spiralling pass out to our winger. The winger draws his man, and he pops me a short pass on the inside. Just like we practised!

I drop my shoulder and launch myself at the first tackler. I bust through him, but the Western Park flankers are both on my tail. And their fullback is racing upfield straight at me!

Without slowing down, I pop a chip kick over the fullback and sprint after it. I catch the ball in the air while I'm still running full pace. There's only ten metres to the goal line. But I feel someone reefing on the back of my jersey.

With five steps to go, a Western Park flanker launches himself at me. He gets both arms locked around my waist. Someone is calling for the ball. Everyone is expecting a famous Sam Brewer offload.

Not this time. I want to prove myself. If I can make it to the goal line, I can win the game.

Just two more steps.

I crash onto the line. I've got two tacklers on me. A third dives on and tries to bash the ball away.

The whistle blasts. "That's a try!" yells the ref.

Air horns blast and the crowd roars. I try to stand up, but the Rebels smother me in a mass bear hug. My try landed right under the posts.

Will boots the conversion straight through the posts. We're up 10–8.

The ref sounds his whistle to end the game.

Try Scored!

Fans flood onto the field. I get a glimpse of Brooke as the guys are pulling me towards the posts for photos. "Way to go, Sam!" she yells. "You rock!"

We take a million team pictures with the Cup. In one of them, I'm sitting in the middle of the team with the Cup on my knees. Just like the picture of Pop all those years ago. *This is the best!* I think. I can't wait to see Pop's face when I hand him the Cup.

Coach Roberts finally gets us all rounded up and into the change room. I'm sitting up front next to Sparrow, right in front of the Cup. It's bigger than I thought. It's three feet tall, and up close I can read the names of all the schools that have won.

"Hundreds of players have fought for the Cup over the years," says Coach Roberts. "It's like a piece of living history."

I think about Pop with the Cup on his lap all those years ago. It makes me shiver.

"Each of you gets five days with her." Coach Roberts places a hand on the top of the Cup. "Time to feel proud of what we achieved today." He points to a sheet of paper taped to the wall. "You'll get your turn in alphabetical order. Anderson will get the Cup for five days, Bittner next, Brewer, Coleman and so on."

It's then that I realize Bittner never got on the field. He's still scowling. He's the only guy with a perfectly clean jersey.

15 LIES

The next day Brooke and I get together in the library. Our social studies project is a great excuse to meet. We sit side by side, and under the table her knee rests against mine.

"I'm wondering," I say. "What if we add something about how homeless camps are popping up all over the country?"

"You were pretty awesome at the game," she says.

I never know what to say when I get a compliment. "Just lucky," I say. "We've got a stellar team."

"And you look super hot out there." She pretends to wipe sweat off her forehead. "Whoa!"

"Oh, yeah," I play along. "That's the only reason I play. Just to look good."

"What's not hot about a muddy guy in short shorts?" She brushes her fingers across my arm. "*And* you won the Cup. You scored the winner!"

"I get the Cup in nine days." I say. "Each guy gets it for five days."

"Nice." Her hand comes to rest on my arm.

"My Pop won it, first year of the Cup," I say. "He's told me about it a million times." Her hand slides to my bicep and her touch is really warm. I feel like I could tell her just about anything.

"I want to see Pop's face," I say, "when I come home with the Cup. That will be the best."

★ ★ ★

I ride the bus home, sitting at the very back. I can't stop daydreaming about Brooke. Maybe she really likes me.

At home I turn my key in the lock, but the door is already open. Mom is standing at the sink. She has her boots and coat on.

"Pop . . ." Her voice is a whisper. "He's missing."

"What do you mean?" I drop my bag.

"Pringle Ridge called. He didn't go to breakfast. No one's seen him all day. I just got a call from the police station. They've opened a file and Pop is considered a missing person."

"Let's go," I blurt. "Let's find him."

Mom chirps the tires of the van pulling out onto the street. We check all the places he used to go. The park, the library, all his favourite coffee shops. We knock on the door of his old duplex and even go to Subway. Then we just drive the streets, looking. I call Pringle Ridge. There's no word on Pop.

We go to the arena where I played hockey. Then we check out the petting zoo he took me to when I was little. At one a.m., we finally hit a drive-through McDonald's. I eat a burger but I don't taste it. I'm exhausted when we get home. It's the middle of the night when I finally get into bed. I don't mind if Pop calls me Dave for the rest of my life. I just want to find him.

The next morning I'm in a deep sleep. I'm dreaming that Sparrow is banging a corner flag into the ground. It's actually someone banging on the front door.

"Hang on," I mumble. I pull on my jeans. Then my stomach lurches in panic. Is the couch still pulled out? What if they see it?

There's more hammering on the door.

Maybe it's about Pop!

The guy at the door has a foot-long nose. "I'm Rick Bittner," he says. "You know my son from school. That's his brother." Mr. Bittner points down the driveway with his thumb.

At the end of our driveway is Bittner's older brother with a dog on a leash. It looks like a Rottweiler mix.

"Where were you late last night?" Mr. Bittner demands. "At two in the morning?"

"I was asleep," I try to explain. "We were up late looking for my Pop."

"A guy who looks just like you was seen leaving our neighbourhood." Mr. Bittner wrinkles up his nose like there's a bad smell.

"What's this about?" I ask.

"Let's look at that old truck." He marches out to the Ford that Pop and I work on. He stands next to the driver's-side window.

The dog is just a few metres away. It follows me with its eyes.

"Have a look." Mr. Bittner uses his thumb and forefinger to make a gun and points at the driver's window.

I see what's on the seat but I don't understand. "That's the Cup."

Mr. Bittner steps right up to me and stabs the finger gun in my chest. "Exactly."

"You stole the Cup from our place." Mr. Bittner's lips curl so I can see his front teeth. He's snarling, just like the dog.

"Someone put it there," I say. "I swear."

"Uh-huh," says Mr. Bittner. "Sure."

"Why would I put the Cup in my truck?" I say.

"Maybe because you didn't think it through," he says. "Maybe because you're not too bright."

Mr. Bittner opens the truck door.

Suddenly I get it. "It was your kid! He's setting me up."

Mr. Bittner doesn't listen. He's rooting around in the truck, looking under the seats and behind the sun visors.

"Oh my, my," he croons. I hear the click of the

glove compartment closing. He has found something. "Look what I've got here."

"What?" I ask.

He holds up an envelope. "My lottery ticket money." Five- and ten-dollar bills are poking out of a big yellow envelope. "And I suppose my son put this in here, too." He stabs the finger gun at me. "Three hundred dollars' worth of golf club lottery money, last seen on my kitchen counter. Principal Renner is going to hear all about this. We're playing eighteen holes tonight, but he's going to hear about it right now." He turns and marches back to their car. Bittner's brother has to yank on the leash to make the dog follow.

I lean against the truck and watch them drive away. As soon as they disappear around the corner, I realize what I have to do. I've got to go to the school and tell the *real* story. Mr. Renner needs to know the truth.

16 Red CARD

I get to school just before the first bell. I hurry to the main office and rush up to the counter. "Excuse me," I say.

But the secretary is pecking at her keyboard. She holds up her hand for me to wait. Finally, she looks up. Her lips are pressed so tight she hardly has a mouth. She looks like she hasn't smiled in a hundred years.

"Can I please see Mr. Renner?" I say. "It's really important."

"Mr. Renner is in a meeting." She starts pecking again.

"When will he be free?" I ask.

She repeats each word on its own, like I'm a child. "He. Is. In. A. Meeting."

"Can I wait?"

She points at the room next to Mr. Renner's office. It's the detention room.

The room has one small window. There's no one in there — just some desks and chairs. I sit in one of the plastic chairs. When the bell rings for class, the secretary walks by and shuts the door on me.

I start thinking about Bittner and my fists clench. And Pop? Where the heck *is* he?

I stand up and start pacing. Back and forth. Three steps to the wall and three steps back. It seems like I've been in here forever.

I really need to prove that Bittner set me up.

I hear Mr. Renner's voice outside the door. He's talking to the secretary and says something to make her laugh. It's more like a cackle. I'm thinking I need to remind her I'm still in here. I pace some more. Back and forth.

The secretary finally opens the door and points for me to go into Mr. Renner's office. He sits behind a desk that's big enough to land a small airplane on. He doesn't invite me to sit. He just looks at me over his glasses. I stand with my hands jammed in my pockets.

"Mr. Brewer," he says, "you have committed a serious offence."

He opens a huge binder and stabs one of the pages with his index finger. "Right here it says that no person who has committed a crime shall be permitted to attend Rosedale Heights. School policy. You don't leave me a lot of choice, Sam."

I'm getting suspended?

Mr. Renner pushes aside the binder. "I'm afraid I'll have to make arrangements for you to finish the year at the Open Door storefront school."

"What about the rugby team?" I plead.

"Sorry, Sam. I'm afraid it's out of the question."

"But I didn't —"

"This is theft," he cuts me off. "It's policy, Sam. We can't allow you to wear the blue and white." He shrugs. "I'm sorry."

My heart sinks. I was expecting a lecture or detentions. Not this.

All the energy drains out of me. I feel wobbly on my legs.

"It is ten o'clock." He looks at his watch. "Start cleaning out your locker. I'll call the storefront school. Let's have it sorted out by eleven."

I shuffle out of his office. I'm numb.

It's between classes and the halls are empty. I ease open the change-room door. The place is deserted. I grab my rugby boots and practice gear from my locker. My Rebels jersey is on a hook. I close the locker door and leave it hanging there.

I grab a few things from my hall locker and stuff them in my bag. Brooke is the only person I want to see. She gets to her locker as the warning bell rings. I lean a shoulder against the locker next to hers.

"Sam!" Her eyes are wide. "Bittner and Dhaliwal are spreading all kinds of ugly rumours."

"I bet," I say.

She glances past me down the hall. "I can't miss Math. Meet me at lunch? In the library?"

"I can't," I tell her. "I got the boot."

Sadness darkens her face. "Really?"

"Not even supposed to be here." I look down at the floor. "Renner gave me an hour to clear out."

"Okay." She slams her locker door. "Downtown." She touches her hand to my arm. "The downtown library. We'll go there." She glances down the hall again. "But I can't be late for class."

I was going to tell her about Pop. But there's no time. I'll wait.

She turns and calls over her shoulder, "Four o'clock?"

"See you then."

There's a ping on my phone. A text from Mom.

they found pop we're at hospital

I run for the back exit of the school.

★ ★ ★

I find Mom on the fourth floor, outside Pop's hospital room. She dabs at her eyes with a balled-up tissue. We hug. Then Mom says, "A dog walker found Pop. He was sitting on the bank of the river at the old Sunday fishing hole."

"Is he okay?" I ask.

"He's very tired. They gave him some medication to help him sleep."

"But is he *okay*?"

"I don't know when he ate last, so they've got him on intravenous for fluids. But yeah, Sam." Mom ruffles my hair like she always does. "He's going to be okay."

I step into Pop's room. The lights are low, and it's quiet except for Pop's even breathing. Pop looks like he's in a deep sleep. His feet stick out from under the thin blanket. They're white as the belly of a fish. I take his big hand in mine. It's warm and I give it a squeeze. I see the trace of a smile, just for a second.

17 Game PLAN

I get to the library at four and find a table by the window. Warm sunlight is slicing through the blinds. Meeting Brooke at school was easy. This is different. I sit down and wipe a trace of sweat from my forehead. I wish I had the guts to ask her out. If my bike wasn't total crap, I could ask her to go for a rip. Maybe we could just go for a hike instead. Or go down to the river for a swim. We'd sit in the sand and dry off in the sun . . .

I'm still daydreaming when she walks through the door. The way she walks, her long legs make my heart skip. She slides into the seat across from me. I tell her the whole story about Mr. Bittner and how he found the Cup and the money in the truck.

"And Renner said no more rugby," I say. "Can you believe it?" I look down at the table. "I feel like a total loser."

"That's harsh." She leans across the table and brushes her fingers across my hand. I love the way she does that.

"We need to find some evidence," she says. "Something that proves Bittner planted that stuff."

"Give me five minutes with the guy." My hands squeeze into fists. "I'd get it out of him."

"Sounds like twenty years for murder." She gives me an exaggerated frown. "I think you're in enough trouble as it is, young man."

"Maybe I could get his geography notebook," I say.

"What for?"

"In class I asked him when I'd get the Cup," I explain. "He wrote in his notebook and showed me. *Don't get your ass in a knot. I'll bring it tomorrow.*"

"That doesn't really prove anything," she says. "But what about his phone? In class he's always texting Dhaliwal. They're like a couple of grade fives." She leans towards me and lowers her voice. "I'll bet any money there are texts about their plan. About planting the Cup in your truck."

"But how do I get my hands on his phone?"

"Maybe *I* could get it." She raises her eyebrows up and down.

The last thing I want is Brooke even talking to Bittner.

My phone rings. "It's Sparrow," I say.

"Go ahead," she says.

"Hey," I say into the phone.

"Sorry, man," says Sparrow. "I heard what

happened. And Roberts called me out of class today. He's all pissy, making sure I get your jersey. Says I have to get it back ASAP. I could come over. Pick it up at your place, if that works."

There's no way I want Sparrow at my place. He probably lives in a mansion. "Don't worry about it," I say. "The jersey is still in my locker. Just grab it. You've got the combo."

We say goodbye and hang up.

"Why does Sparrow have your locker combo?" Brooke places her hands flat on the table. Her fingers are just centimetres from mine.

"Just my gym locker." I inch my fingers closer to hers. "Because he's the manager. He's got everyone's combo."

Brooke cocks her head and squints her eyes. I can tell she's got an idea.

"What?" I place one of my hands on hers.

"I know how to get a look at Bittner's phone." She turns her hands upward.

Now we're holding hands.

"PE class," she says. "It's the one time Bittner's phone won't be in his pocket. We need Sparrow on board." She gives my hand a little squeeze. "Sparrow is the key."

It takes me a minute. I'm totally distracted by our hands, but finally I get it. I call Sparrow right back.

"Remember the first time we met?" I ask him. "At Pinky's Laundromat?"

"Sure," he says, "I remember. That guy wanted to give me plastic surgery with a coat hanger."

"You said you owe me one."

"You bet," says Sparrow.

"C Block is Bittner's PE class," I explain. "It's the one time he won't have his phone. It'll be in his PE locker. If I can get in his locker, I'll take screen shots of the texts he sent to Dhaliwal. I'm positive they talked about setting me up."

"So you need Bittner's combo?" Sparrow asks. "Give me a sec."

I hear him rustling papers. He's probably flipping through one of his clipboards.

"Right here," he says.

I write down the numbers. Fifteen, twenty-four, eleven. "Thanks, Sparrow."

Now the plan is simple.

★ ★ ★

When I get home, Mom is at the stove cooking her famous hash browns. The smell of fried margarine and onions makes my mouth water.

"Pop's awake," Mom says.

"When can I see him?"

"Anytime, I guess. But just a short visit. Don't wear the poor old guy out." She tosses a handful of chopped celery into the pan. "We talked for a while and he asked about you. He knew where he was and who I was."

I put plates on the table and get a jug of milk from the fridge.

"We were having a good talk," she says. "But then I lost him. He started talking about painting a barn."

"When can I see him?" I ask again.

"In the morning," she says. "Best if he gets some rest. You can go early if you want."

I decide I'll go first thing in the morning. I put salt and pepper on the table and look for the hot sauce. We're out. There are just a few packets of ketchup in the fridge door. Mom fries eggs to go with the hash browns. There was a time that I'd have complained and asked where the meat was. Not anymore.

18 BUSTED

It's early the next morning when I get to the hospital. I need to keep an eye on the clock. I've got to get to the school in time for C Block and Bittner's PE class.

Pop is awake and sitting up in bed. He still has a tube poked in his arm. A crop of white chest hair sticks out of his pajama top. At first he doesn't see me. He's holding a bowl of green Jell-O up to his nose.

"Hi, Pop," I say from the end of the bed.

"Don't even try it, Mister." He points a finger at me. "I'm not taking another pill or any of your snake-oil potion."

"I'm Sam," I say. "Your grandson."

He looks me up and down then holds out the Jell-O. "Smell this," he says.

I take a whiff. "Smells okay to me."

You never know around here," he says. "Last night they left the gate open and the dogs got out." He points a finger at me again. "Took me half the night to round them up."

"Can I get you anything?" I ask.

"Just make sure the dogs are fed." He spoons a bit of Jell-O out of the bowl and holds it up to the light.

"You bet," I say. It rips me apart to see Pop like this.

A nurse steps in the door. She has kind eyes. "You okay?" she asks.

I nod and wipe my eye with the heel of my hand. "I'm good."

"How are we today?" she asks Pop.

"I'm not going to eat this." He holds the spoon towards her.

"How's he been?" I ask the nurse.

"Had a few crystal-clear moments last night. Asked about you and your mom." She's looking at Pop's chart. "Mostly he's in and out."

"Are you going to tell me what you people put in this stuff?" Pop has dumped the spoon of Jell-O into his hand. He holds it close to examine it.

The nurse says, "You might need to get some rest, my dear." I think she's giving me an excuse to leave.

"See you, Pop," I say. "I'll come back later with Mom."

"She's been in the boat all morning." He's dropped the Jell-O back in the bowl and he's wiping his hand on the sheets. "Tell her to wear a life jacket."

I wish he were the old Pop that I could lean on. If ever I needed him, I need him now.

Busted

It feels like rain when I get off the bus a block from the school. Only thirty minutes until C block ends. My heart is thumping. My pits are soaked with cold sweat. I'm walking towards the back of the school and I've got the nervous puke feeling again.

Three storeys of windows are looking down at me. If the wrong person looks down and sees me, I'm done.

I pull the back door open and quickly slip inside. The hallway is deserted, and all the classroom doors are shut. With each step, the squeak of my runners echoes off the walls. I sneak past the gym and the heavy thump of basketballs. I put my hand on the change-room door. I'm about to push it open when I hear footsteps. Someone is coming around the corner. I pull out my phone and pretend I'm texting. The janitor shuffles around the corner, pushing a dust mop.

"Morning, Sam," he says and sweeps right past.

"Morning, Mr. Thomas." I nod and try to smile.

He must be the only person in the whole place who doesn't know the story. *Or maybe he does*, I worry.

I shove the door open. The change room is deserted. I need to get into Bittner's locker, grab his phone and find the texts. I just wish Mr. Thomas hadn't seen me. He might be on his way to the office. Renner could be down here in a flash.

The gym is right next door, and the thump of bouncing basketballs pounds through the wall. I go straight to Bittner's locker and start to spin his three-number combo. My heart races but my fingers seem to move in slow motion. I tug on the lock. It doesn't open. I slow down and try the numbers once more. Clockwise to fifteen, backwards to twenty-four. It's taking forever. I spin the dial back to eleven, yank on the lock, and it finally snaps open.

Bittner's jeans are hanging on a hook, with his phone in the back pocket. I slip the phone out and press Home. I'm in luck — there's no password to enter. Then I hit the messaging icon. Dhaliwal's name is right there. I scroll through a million of their texts. Sweat trickles down my temple. The messages between Bittner and Dhaliwal seem to go on forever.

From the gym there's a sharp blast of Coach Roberts's whistle. The balls stop bouncing. I freeze. It sounds like he's shouting some kind of instructions.

Finally, I find what I'm looking for.

Dhaliwal's text: *did it work?*

Bittner: *hell ya!!! Brewers busted*

Dhaliwal: *awesome!*

Bittner: *tossed dads lottery $ in the glove compartment — 300 bucks!*

Dhaliwal: *genius!!!!*

I need to take screen shots and send them to my phone. There are more texts about me going to jail. Bittner says I'll probably like it.

I stop and listen. It's completely quiet in the gym. I wonder what's going on. I hear footsteps in the hall, then there's a rumble of voices right outside the door! I glance at the back of the room. Maybe I should hide in a cubicle.

The change-room door flies open. I stuff Bittner's phone in my pocket. A dozen guys flood into the change room. I'm standing in front of Bittner's open locker with his lock in my hand.

19 RUN!

"What the hell!" yells Bittner.

The whole gang stops. No one says a word.

"Get him!" yells Dhaliwal.

Before I can take a step, half a dozen guys are on me. Bittner throws a powerhouse punch that smashes my cheek. My head snaps back and for a second, I see black. Hands are yanking and tearing at me. I fall to my knees. Dhaliwal's boot thuds my chest dead centre. I'm driven to the ground. My arms and legs are pinned. Bittner has me by the collar.

"You're busted, Ghetto," he says. He's so close I can smell his sour breath. He jams a fist under my chin. "Make a move and you're done."

"What the heck is going on?" Coach Roberts yells from the door.

"Brewer's busting into lockers," Dhaliwal blurts. "Looking for cash."

Coach Roberts pushes his way through and pulls me to my feet. My shirt has a spatter of blood down the front, and half the buttons are ripped off. He takes me by the elbow and we head for the door. My face is throbbing like I've been hit with a bat.

"We caught him red-handed," says Dhaliwal.

"He was in my locker." Bittner holds the locker door open like it's proof.

Coach Roberts holds up a hand to stop the talk. "I've got it from here, boys." He keeps his grip on my elbow and steers me out the door.

Bittner gets the last shot in. "Hope you get a hillbilly cellmate," he hollers. There are a few snorting laughs.

Coach Roberts takes me into the main office and points to the chairs near the door. I sit and pinch my nostrils together to stop a trickle of blood. I touch my index finger under my eye. It's already puffing up.

Coach Roberts disappears into Renner's office. I hear him explain through the open door, "I dismissed my PE class early. I'd finished testing." I strain to hear more.

Mr. Renner comes to his door and locks eyes with me. "You are getting deeper and deeper in trouble, Mr. Brewer." He points a finger at me. "Sit tight, young man, while we sort this mess out." He goes back in his office, and this time he shuts the door. The secretary looks over top of her glasses at me and shakes her head.

The bell rings to end the class. Bittner starts lurking out in the hall with a few buddies. He's smirking. He pats his back pocket. Then he pats his front pockets. His smirk turns to worry. Then panic.

"My phone!" he howls. "He's got my phone!"

I tear open the office door and bolt out. Dozens of students are flooding into the hallways. I run. There's a swarm of kids between me and Bittner.

"Get him!" shouts Bittner.

I sprint down the hall. A group of girls are in the way. I swerve to get past, lose my footing and crash a shoulder into the lockers.

"Catch him!" Bittner is racing after me. Dhaliwal and two others are right behind him, bashing through the crowd.

I skid around a corner and shove a big guy out of the way. I shoulder through a couple of others. Mr. Morris comes out of his classroom with a bunch of books on a steel cart. He doesn't see me and wheels right into my path. With my hands out front, I hit the cart. It crashes down and all the books spill across the floor. I keep running.

A few metres back, Bittner slips on a book and goes down hard on the floor. The next guy stumbles and falls over him.

I race around the corner. But as soon as I'm out of Bittner's sight, I slow to a walk like I'm just another kid on my way to class. I walk a few steps, then push open the door to the boy's bathroom. Two guys have their backs to me at the urinals. I step into the last stall, sit down and lock the door. My breath is coming in long gasps.

One urinal flushes. Then the other. The door opens and closes.

I'm alone.

I feel the bulge of Bittner's phone in my pocket. That's the proof. But a quick delete and poof, it would be gone. I wonder if I could trust Mr. Renner.

There's only one person who can help me out. Coach Kanavula. I think he said he was assigned to an elementary school. P. T. Phelps. It's across town.

The noise in the hallway fades. In few minutes, all I can hear is the dull hum of the heating system. It's time to escape.

Two bus rides later, it's lunchtime at P. T. Phelps. From half a block away I can hear the babble and laughter of little kids. Coach Kanavula is at one end of the playground with a gaggle of kids chasing a ball.

I slip through the playground gate as the bell rings. All the kids run for the school doors.

"Hey, Coach," I say.

"Sam," he says, frowning, "you look a bit of a mess."

I've forgotten that my shirt is blood-spattered, with half the buttons ripped off. I touch my cheek and realize I have a gold-ribbon black eye shaping up.

I babble out the whole story. Then I hand Coach Kanavula the phone, open to Bittner's texts.

Coach Kanavula scans through the texts. "It says right here that he planted the money in your truck."

"Can you help?" I ask.

"I know Renner pretty well. And Roberts and I go way back." He rubs a hand over the stubble on his chin. "I'll get to the bottom of this."

20 The AGREEMENT

The next day Coach Kanavula meets with Mr. Renner and Coach Roberts. He shows them the texts. They decide there should be a "mediation" meeting. It's for me, Dhaliwal and Bittner to get past our differences. Mr. Morris, a school counsellor, will run it. I decide I'm only going to go to this mediation thing because I have to. But I can't see what good it's going to do. *One big meeting is supposed to fix things?* I wonder.

★ ★ ★

When I step up to Mr. Morris's office door, the others are already there inside. Mr. Morris waves me in, and I sit on the edge of one of the padded chairs. No one is speaking. Mr. Morris, Bittner, Dhaliwal and I sit in a tight circle. I'm centimetres from Bittner. My heart thumps.

Bright sun slivers through the blinds. Outside, the hum of a lawn mower in the distance tries to make the place seem peaceful.

Dhaliwal is rolling a steel water bottle between his palms at high speed. He's watching it go back and forth. I'm thinking that he'll wait for Bittner's lead. Like always. But a second glance tells me he looks super nervous. If he presses the water bottle any tighter, it's going to bust.

Bittner has his arms folded across his chest. I figure he's going to just sit there and be his butt-head self. That or tell a few more lies. But a closer look tells me he's stressed, too. One knee is bobbing and the pits of his shirt are dark with sweat.

"We don't have a lot of choice here, boys," says Mr. Morris. "I know the full story and we need full participation. From all of you."

I feel sweat beading on my forehead.

"I'm not saying you have to walk out of here best buddies," says Mr. Morris. "But all three of you need to be honest today. Honest with me. Honest with each other." He takes off his glasses and carefully polishes the lenses with a tissue.

"Honest about what?" asks Dhaliwal.

"Good question, Kuldeep," replies Mr. Morris. "I'm going to ask some tough questions." He puts his glasses back on. "And they need to be answered. All of them."

Dhaliwal squirms in his seat. His mouth hangs open like it does when he's thinking hard. Bittner looks at his fingernails like suddenly they're the most important thing in the world. I realize my shoulder muscles are totally tight.

"Let's make the first question an easy one," says Mr. Morris. "Why do you play rugby?"

I love the game. But it's hard to find the right words under pressure.

"The hits," Bittner says. "I love tackling. That's why I'm a flanker."

I'm surprised. Bittner is going to take part.

"Thanks for getting us started, Shawn," says Mr. Morris.

I forgot his name was Shawn. Even the teachers call him Bittner.

Mr. Morris lets us sit in silence. I'm not good with silence.

"Same with me," I say. "I like how physical the game is. And I love running with the ball."

"Friends," Dhaliwal suddenly blurts. "To make friends."

"Friends." Mr. Morris says. "And how does that work?"

Dhaliwal keeps rolling the bottle between his palms. Back and forth. "I didn't want to get hacked on. So I joined rugby to make friends." He's straight-faced. He seems legit.

"It's easy to make friends in rugby?" Mr. Morris asks us.

There's another awkward silence. Mr. Morris's clock ticks on the shelf.

"Yeah," says Bittner. "I've played a lot of sports.

But rugby is different. It's kind of . . ." he shrugs.

"It's like a brotherhood," I say. "I don't know why, maybe because it's so physical. But guys who play rugby are tight. There's, like, a rugby bond."

"That doesn't seem to be the case here," says Mr. Morris.

No kidding, I think.

"We need to find the root of the problem," says Mr. Morris. "What caused this whole thing to —"

Dhaliwal breaks in. "Shawn is my *one* friend. It's not easy being an Indo kid. And when we started teasing Sam, he was new and it seemed like a normal thing to do." He glances across the circle at me.

"Shawn?" Mr. Morris asks.

Outside, the lawn mower has gone silent. The clock ticks. A bead of sweat trickles down my temple.

Bittner is looking at his shoes. "I heard Sam was coming to the Rebels," he starts in a hushed voice. "I knew it would be a fight for the number seven jersey. Open-side flanker." He glances at me. "That's always been my spot. Guys on the team, Coach Roberts, they always say I rock getting to the breakdown, stealing the ball."

"It was an idiot move," Dhaliwal jumps in. "Teasing Sam, setting him up, the whole thing. We're supposed to be a team, but —"

Bittner cuts him off. "So I was freaked. When I heard Sam Brewer was coming up, I knew I was in trouble. Specially with a sprained wrist. I'd seen you play, Sam." Bittner looks right at me. "I knew the jersey would be up for grabs."

I meet Bittner's eyes. I'm surprised to see they're not full of anger.

I think it's my turn to say something, but Mr. Morris saves me.

"So where do we go from here?" he asks.

"What do you mean?" asks Dhaliwal.

Mr. Morris leans back and lets us think about it. A breeze comes in the window and rattles the blinds.

I think of all the advice Pop has given me over the years. "I'll do whatever it takes," I say. My voice isn't much more than a whisper.

I expect Mr. Morris to say something. He doesn't. He lets the silence linger again. But from the corner of my eye I see he's looking at me. I guess it's my turn.

I turn towards Shawn. "I had to steal your phone," I say. "It was —"

"I know." He meets my eyes again. "It's what I would have done in your shoes. I thought setting you up was my only way out. You know, way back in the first intersquad, *I* told Kuldeep to give you a cheap shot. I thought you might wuss out, but you didn't. I guess . . ." Bittner doesn't finish. He looks down and shakes his head.

"Go on, Shawn," says Mr. Morris.

Bittner glances around the circle. He sucks in a

huge breath and says, "If anybody should ride the pine in the England game, I guess it should be me."

I can't help but wonder, *Is Shawn just saying what Mr. Morris wants to hear?*

Then Dhaliwal surprises me. "Sorry, Sam," he says. He holds his hand out to me.

I hesitate a second. Then I give his hand a firm shake. I think of Pop again. What would he want me to do next?

I extend my hand to Shawn Bittner.

21 The Secret IS OUT

A couple of days later, I'm sitting in the hospital waiting area. I've finally got the Quinton Cup. It looks huge on my lap, and everyone who passes by gives me a smile.

The minute visiting hours officially start, I open Pop's door. There are two other old guys in his room. The curtains are pulled around their beds, but I can hear someone snoring like a freight train. Behind the other curtain is the murmur of a game show on TV. Pop is propped up on a stack of pillows, fast asleep.

I place the Cup on the chair next to Pop's bed. He looks way better than he did a few days ago. A cozy blanket has him all covered up. The tubes are gone and there's colour back in his face.

"Hey, Pop?" I touch a hand to his shoulder.

Pop's eyelids flutter for a second. Then they slowly open. He smiles. "Hey, Sam."

"Can I get you anything?" I ask.

"A drink of water would be . . ." Pop stops mid-sentence. He sees the Cup.

I pick it up and set it on the edge of his bed.

"That's the Cup!" Pop uses his elbows to inch himself upright. "The Quinton Cup!" He stares at it, wide-eyed.

"We beat Western Park in the final," I remind him.

"And you scored the winner." He strokes his finger along the wooden base of the Cup. "Never thought I'd see the day. You must have a heck of a team."

"You bet." I decide to tell Pop what I've been thinking. "But you know what? It's only in the last little while that I even feel like I'm *part* of that team."

"I wondered how that would go." Pop uses his elbows again to push his way up and sit tall. "Up there among all those rich kids." His eyes are clear and I can tell he's totally with it. "But what you're going through is normal. Takes a while to fit in."

"You always talk about the brotherhood and all that," I say.

"The brotherhood is out there. It always will be," he says. "This is just one team. You've got a whole lifetime of rugby ahead of you."

"I shook hands with Shawn Bittner," I say. "To make peace. And my gut feeling is it might have worked."

Pop reaches over and places his big square hand on my shoulder. He looks me straight in the eye. "It takes a big man to do what you did." There's a tear in his eye.

I know there won't be many more times like this.

Pop's dementia isn't going to get better. But right now he's totally with it and his eyes are smiling. This is a moment I need to remember. Always.

★ ★ ★

The next morning I'm out in our driveway. The street is quiet and the crappy weather has finally blown over. The sun is peeking in and out of white clouds.

The old truck's door creaks when I pull it open. Inside is the same old wet-carpet smell as always. I turn the key, but there's nothing. Just a click. I pop the hood and disconnect the battery. Pop showed me how to clean the battery terminals. I scrub away at them with a tough little wire brush. Then I scrub the connectors.

It's Saturday, so Mom is still sleeping. When she gets up, we'll try a jump-start. I come out from under the hood and something catches my eye. Halfway down the block there's a girl pushing her bike.

It's Brooke!

Mom is still sleeping. On the pullout! I can't let Brooke see.

Brooke is walking my way. I feel a surge of panic and duck back behind the truck. She hasn't seen me yet. I watch her through the truck windows. It looks like she's limping. There's no time to hide the pullout. Brooke is getting closer. Then I see blood streaked down one of her shins.

"Hey, Brooke." I step out from behind the truck.

"Sam!" Her eyes open wide in surprise. "What are you —"

"What happened?" I take a close look at her leg. There's a deep scrape torn across her knee.

"My chain broke." She gently touches the wound. "I wiped out."

I swallow hard and say something I thought I'd never say. "Want to come inside?" I'm not sure how this is going to go, but I start walking towards our door. "Come on."

Brooke is going to see Mom sleeping on the pullout. It's going to be awkward.

I get to the bottom of the stairs and open the door. The smell of fresh-brewed coffee fills the kitchen. Mom is at the counter.

"This is Brooke," I tell my mom. I pull out a chair for Brooke to sit at the kitchen table.

"Hi, Brooke." Mom beams a smile, then gets a look at Brooke's knee. "What happened?"

"My chain broke." Brooke rolls her eyes. "Then I slipped off the pedal and *crash*. Total fail."

"I've got a first-aid kit." Mom pours Brooke a mug of apple juice. She gets down on one knee to examine the wound. "It's in the van, Sam."

When I come back with the kit, Mom and Brooke are laughing. Mom patches up Brooke with a big square bandage and a lot of tape.

Mom looks at her watch. "I've got to get going." She drains the last of her coffee. "Tallman and Schuster just called. I got it!" Mom throws me a high five. "Nice to meet you, Brooke." Mom pops out the door and takes the stairs two at a time.

"Mom got a new contract," I explain. "It's a pretty big deal."

Brooke is looking into the living room. Mom has left the pullout bed a mess. She must have been in a giant rush. There's a twist of sheets and blankets hanging off one side. Pillows are stacked one on top of the other. They've never looked so big and obvious.

Brooke sips her juice.

I might as well just tell her. "My mom sleeps there," I blurt.

Brooke walks into the living room and stands right at the foot of the pullout. I never thought this would happen. I feel ashamed. Then I feel bad about feeling ashamed.

"Same as my aunt's place," Brooke says. "You just pick up one end." She lifts the end of the bed a foot off the floor. "And it slides in. Right?"

"Right." I put a hand on her elbow. I need to get her back into the kitchen.

But she tosses one of Mom's pillows onto the coffee table. "I'll help," she says as she straightens the blankets. "I slept on one of these for a whole summer." She pats the mattress. "Pretty comfy."

"You did?" I straighten the blankets on my side.

Brooke stretches the sheets nice and tight. She smiles like it's no big deal.

I smile back.

Together we grab the end of the bed and slide it in. Brooke grabs the couch cushions and stuffs them in place. Then she plops down and pats a cushion for me to sit down, too.

I sit next to her.

"Just like that." She rests a hand on mine. "All done."

22 Never PROUDER

On game day, the team is in the change room an hour before kickoff. We're at University Stadium and the change room is huge. The clack of cleats on the cement floor echoes off the walls. The spicy smell of Deep Heat hangs in the air. I'm wrapping tape around my laces like I always do. Four wraps on each boot. Halfway through the second boot, my tape runs out.

Bittner is sitting across from me. I look at him and wait to catch his eye. "Got any tape?" I hold up my empty roll. I'm not sure what he'll say. This is a test.

He turns away. I think he's ignoring me. But he's turned to dig in his bag. He tosses me the end of a roll.

"I always tape the left boot first, too." He nods down at my boots. "Superstition," he says. "It's good luck."

"We're going to *need* some luck." I start wrapping his tape around my right boot.

"I'll tell you what, Sam." He stands up. "We'll be at the breakdown so fast, me and you, those English boys

115

won't know what hit them." He gives me a thumbs-up and walks towards the toilets.

Me and you. He said it like we're a team.

On the field, the corner flags snap in the breeze. The pitch is perfectly lined. I get a sharp whiff of cut grass. A big yellow sun is right overhead in a perfectly clear sky.

The parking lot is jammed full. A couple of police are trying to direct traffic. Cars are parking almost a kilometre down the street. We're opening for the senior game, and half the town has tickets. The newspaper and Channel 10 are here. Outside the gates, the food trucks are parked side by side. The sweet smell of fried onions wafts from the hotdog stand. A couple of kids are shouting over the thump of the music, "Programs! Get your programs here!"

Programs? Really? I marvel. I've only ever dreamed of being in a program. But there I am! There's a picture of each player with his position, height, weight and a little space to answer the question, *Why do you play rugby?*

It's a game of opposites, I wrote. *It's hard-hitting and fierce, but underneath there's respect, brotherhood and love of the game.*

As the game is about to start, both teams line up along the sidelines. Our blue-and-white uniforms are spotless and crisp. We've rehearsed this part. The Bedford team is lined up in their royal red and gold.

Together we face the grandstands. All the fans are standing. Our school choir is backed up by the local men's choir. "God Save the Queen" booms across the grounds. Then, when the first notes of "O Canada" start up, I join in. I can't help myself. I'm not a great singer, but all the voices ramp me up. A pair of RCMP officers hold our flags. England and Canada fly side by side.

Then I spot Pop. He's only a few days out of hospital, but he insisted on being here. Pop is standing at attention. He has a hand on his heart, and I can see that he is singing. For a second, it's like I can hear his voice above all the others.

I close my eyes and sing my heart out. "O Canada, we stand on guard for thee."

Right from the whistle, the English team hammers us hard with their forwards. A big lock charges forward. He takes an ankle tackle, goes to ground and the next couple of players drive us off the ball. Then one of their props picks up from the back of the ruck. He drives a couple of metres, hits the turf and they drive us off again. They pick and drive off every ruck.

It's exhausting work. They're driving us back. Metre by metre.

Finally, they spin the ball wide and try to outpace our backs. Somehow we hold our ground, and the crowd roars every time we make a big tackle.

The school band's bass drum thumps. A trumpet

blasts the notes to charge. *Ta-Ta-Ta Tum Ta-Tum* — "Charge!" yells the crowd. But all we can do is scramble to hold our defensive line and make desperate tackles.

Our defence pays off. Brandon Wells makes a thundering hit on their fly-half and the little Brit knocks the ball on.

The whistle tweets. "Rosedale scrum!" shouts the ref.

"Nice tackle, Brandon." I thump him on the back. But Brandon has a bloody nose and needs a sub. When water comes on the field, all of us are glad to suck a few big breaths.

"Twenty-three blue!" Coach Roberts yells from the sideline.

Our team knows the play inside out. It's a simple exit play to get the ball out of our own end. First we have to win our scrum. Then Will Nakamura will be kicking downfield for the touchline. With any luck, we'll force the English boys back to midfield for a line-out.

The scrum sets with a mighty surge. We win the hook and channel the ball with our feet back to the number eight. Will is set up deep behind our scrum. He gets a good long pass from our scrum-half and puts up a high kick. It catches the breeze. Our fastest backs fly downfield. I charge forward with them.

The English winger calls, "My ball!" But our blue jerseys are right there on him. He takes his eye off the ball, and it bounces off his chest. Our fullback, Matt Romano, snatches the ball out of the air. He fires me a long infield pass.

I lunge forward and catch the ball at my bootlaces. I'm back up just in time to meet the first tackler. He comes in high, arms reaching out. I hit him with an explosive straight-arm and he stumbles back. I bust into high gear and glimpse the goal line twenty metres away. A defender clamps one hand on the back of my shorts. Another tackler launches himself, gets both arms around me and smothers the ball.

"Sam! Sam!" There's a support player on my heels. But there are arms grabbing all over me. I plow forward and wrench myself sideways, trying to rip the ball free of the clutching arms. The tacklers are hauling me down.

"Sam!" I hear. "I'm on your right!"

Just as I'm crashing to the turf, I manage a one-hand pass. A perfect Sam Brewer offload.

My teammate makes the catch. He sprints across open ground, racing for the posts. Five metres out, he dives over the try-line and scores!

It's Bittner.

The entire crowd leaps to their feet. The whole place roars with applause.

"Beauty offload, Sam!" Will gives me a mighty chest bump.

Our team rushes in to mob us under the posts. The

guys are bouncing off each other like we've won the World Cup.

Bittner throws an arm over my shoulders. "What a pass!" he shouts. "Amazing." And he's not being sarcastic. He's for real.

I can't help but feel good about it. It *was* one of my best offloads ever. But the best thing is that I'm okay with Bittner. It's totally okay that *he* scored our try.

I get a glimpse of Pop up in the bleachers. He's standing with his hands clamped together on his chest, like he's praying for something. But Pop doesn't have to worry. For the first time in weeks I feel like I'm getting it back. The *team* feeling.

I get a warm rush of emotion that fills me up from head to toe. I know what Pop would say about it. He'd say it comes from the love of the game. The brotherhood.

ABOUT RUGBY

The primary objective of a rugby game is to score more points than the opposition.

POINTS

There are four ways to score points. A **try** is worth five points. To score a try, a player runs across the opposition's goal line and touches the ball to the ground. When a try is scored, a **conversion kick** is attempted. It must be taken directly back from the point where the try was scored and is worth two points. A **penalty kick** is worth three points. When a team commits an offence, the opposition gets a penalty kick at goal from where the offence occurred; if it goes through the posts, three points are awarded. At any time, and from anywhere on the field, a player can attempt a **drop goal**. The player drops the ball to ground and, as it bounces up, kicks it through the posts. A drop goal is worth three points.

PASSING

Players may never throw the ball forward. They can run as far as they like with ball in hand or kick the ball forward and chase it.

PLAYERS

Each team has fifteen players. There are eight forwards (also known as scrummers) and seven backs. The number on the player's jersey indicates the position he or she is playing.

Props (numbers 1 and 3): In a set scrum, the prop's job is to hold up the weight of the hooker, keep the scrum from collapsing and move the scrum forward. In open-field play, props are often used as battering rams that crash straight upfield. They typically receive short passes and run short distances into contact.

Hooker (number 2): The hooker's job in a set scrum is to hook, using the feet, to win possession of the ball. In a line-out, the hooker is typically responsible for the throw-in.

Locks or second row (numbers 4 and 5): In the set scrum, the locks are sometimes referred to as the engine room. Their job is to drive the scrum forward. In open-field play, they are hard running players who are often difficult to take down.

Blind-side flanker (number 6): The blind-side flanker binds onto the side of the scrum that is farthest from the string of backs. This player's job is to break from the scrum as soon as the ball is out and support their players with the ball, tackle the opposition or try to win possession of the ball at the breakdown.

Open-side flanker (number 7): In the set scrum, the open-side flanker binds on the side nearest to the back line. This player's job is to break from the scrum quickly and try to win the ball at the breakdown.

Number eight (number 8): The number eight binds at the very back of the scrum. When the ball has been channelled to the back of the scrum, the number eight often controls it with the feet until the scrum-half picks it up.

Scrum-half (number 9): The scrum-half is the connection between the forwards and the backs. Often the scrum-half directs traffic on the field by telling support players where they should go to be most effective.

Fly-half (number 10): The fly-half is often the most important playmaker on the field and is usually the first player to receive the ball from the scrum-half. The fly-half typically directs the back line. The fly-half is usually the best open-field kicker and is often the team's goal kicker as well.

Wings (numbers 11 and 14): There is a left and right wing, often the team's fastest runners. A wing is usually at the end of the back line and a finisher on offence.

Inside centre (number 12): The inside centre lines up in the back line outside the fly-half. A good inside centre is a powerful runner who is often used to punch holes in the defensive line.

Outside centre (number 13): In the back line, the outside centre lines up outside the inside centre. The outside centre uses speed and agility to attack the defensive line.

Fullback (number 15): The fullback often lines up behind the back line and is often the last line of defence. The fullback is often responsible for catching high-kicked balls.

GLOSSARY

BREAKDOWN: Occurs when a player is tackled and both teams fight for possession of the ball. The breakdown usually ends when a player gets possession.

CARDS: A player may be given a card by the referee for a serious and dangerous offense. A player who is given a yellow card is sent off the field for ten minutes. A player who is given a red card is sent off the field for the rest of the game.

CHIP KICK: A short kick intended to go over the heads of the defenders, to be regathered by the kicker's team.

HIGH TACKLE: An illegal tackle in which the tackler grabs the opponent above the shoulders, around the neck or head. It could result in a penalty, a yellow card or a red card.

LATE TACKLE/HIT: A tackle in which a player tackles another player after that player has passed or kicked the ball away. It is illegal to tackle or block any player who is not in possession of the ball.

LINE-OUT: Used to restart the game when the ball has gone out of bounds. The forwards from each team line up facing each other. The hooker throws the ball into the space between the two teams, and both teams compete to catch it.

OFFLOAD: When a player being tackled can get a pass away to a teammate before the tackle is completed and the player hits the ground.

PENALTY KICK: When a team commits an illegal act, the opposition can attempt a penalty kick from the spot where the penalty occurred.

SUPPORT PLAYERS: Players behind and within passing distance of a teammate who has the ball in hand.

SCRUM: Used to restart the game after an infringement. The players from each team crouch, bind onto one another and meet shoulder to shoulder with the front row of the opposition scrum. The ball is rolled into the "tunnel" between the two teams. The objective is to win the ball by driving the scrum forward and moving the ball to the back of the scrum with the feet.

SCRUMMER: Another name for a forward or a player who takes part in the scrum.

Glossary

TRY: The primary method of scoring. A try is scored when a player is able to cross the opposition's goal line and touch the ball to the ground.

ACKNOWLEDGEMENTS

A huge thank you to Kat Mototsune for her ideas, her expertise, and for walking me through all the stages of editing.